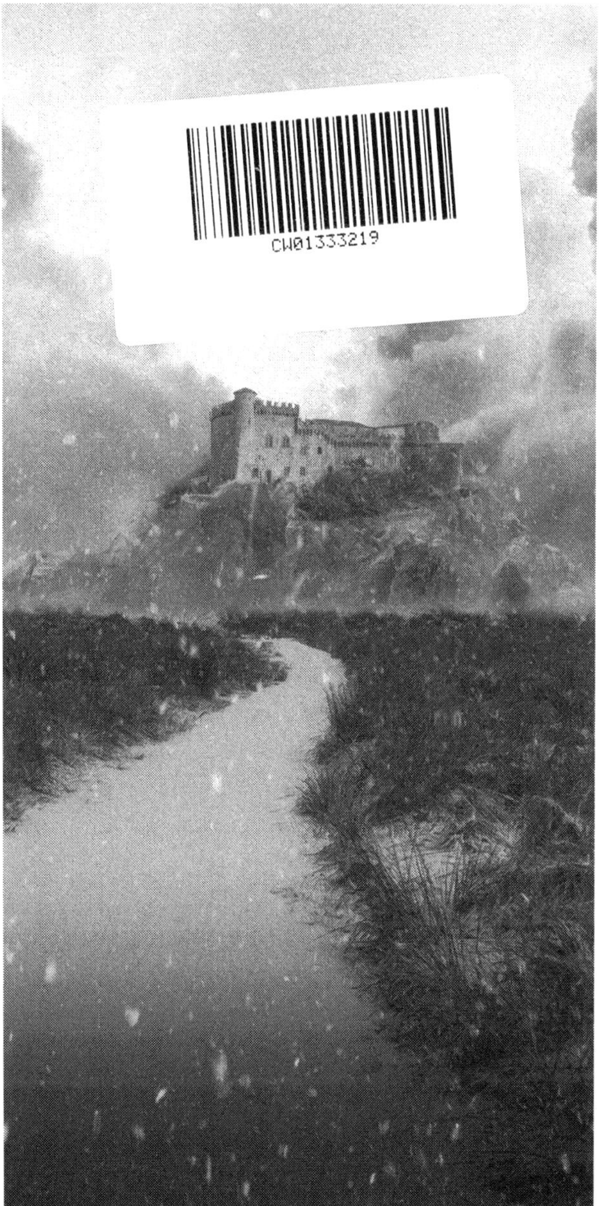

YULETIDE ANGELS
THE CLAN GRANT, BOOK 9
Published by Keira Montclair
Copyright © 2021 by Keira Montclair

All rights reserved. Except for use in any review, the reproduction or utilization of this work in whole or in part in any form by any electronic, mechanical or other means, now known or hereinafter invented, including xerography, photocopying and recording, or in any information storage or retrieval system, is forbidden without the written permission of the publisher.

This is a work of fiction. Names, characters, places and incidents are either the product of the author's imagination or are used fictitiously, and any resemblance to actual persons, living or dead, business establishments, events or locales is entirely coincidental.

Printed in the USA.

Cover Design and Interior Format
© KILLION
THE GROUP, INC.

Yuletide ANGELS

THE CLAN GRANT SERIES
BOOK NINE

MADDIE & ALEX

KEIRA MONTCLAIR

To my readers:
Merry Christmas!
Happy Holidays!
This wee tale takes place after the Battle of Largs, when Alex and Maddie's family is young and still growing. It should be Book 5 in the series by timeline, but I made it Book 9 because it's a novella.
I have often been asked, "What happens after the wedding?"
Here's a short answer for you.
Enjoy my brief visit into your two favorite characters' younger days.
And remember, you sometimes just have to believe in something that seems impossible.
'Tis the season for miracles.

CHAPTER ONE

December 1263
The Highlands of Scotland, Grant Castle

MADELINE GRANT CHASED after her two lads, who were play-fighting with their wooden swords. Jake and Jamie—twins, nearly four winters old—were often a bit too enthusiastic in their imitation of battle.

Jake swung his sword, knocking Jamie's out of his hand. "I kill the Norse who attack our land."

"I'm not a Norseman. I'm a Scot too!" Jamie snatched up his sword from the ground. "I will send them running from the beach. Then I'll get my slinger and shoot the stones at their foreheads."

Jake laughed. "Loki's slinger is in my hand, not yours. He gave me one."

Jamie fought back. "And I wear my chain mail and send the Norse running from the beach." Then Jake swung his sword hard against his brother's weapon, sending the sword flying through the air once again.

"Jake, stop!"

"Die, Norseman!" Jake swung again, this time catching his brother's wrist as he reached for the wooden handle of his weapon.

Jamie cried out in pain. "Mama, Jake hit me."

"Stop crying, you wee bairn. Warriors don't cry." Jake dropped his sword to the ground and crossed his arms in a stance that showed a strong imitation of his sire.

"Lads, please do not strike each other and cease your arguing." Maddie paused, adjusting the babe she was carrying. "Or you will upset your sister."

"Aye, Mama," Jamie sniffled.

"Mama, we must practice battle to be as good as our sire," Jake explained, leaning down to pick up his weapon before turning to Jamie again. "I attack you, Norseman. I have my golden helm on."

His weapon over his head, his mother barked, "John Alexander Grant." Then Maddie set Kyla down and took both swords away. "If you cannot play nicely with them, you cannot have them." Though they were twins, the two didn't look at all alike. Jake had dark hair and gray eyes like Alex, while Jamie had Maddie's blonde hair and blue eyes. Kyla was a lovely mix, with Alex's nearly black locks and her mother's blue eyes.

Jake whined, "But Mama, 'tis a war, a big battle with the Norse, just like Papa and Uncle Brodie and Uncle Robbie fought."

"And Papa did not hurt Uncle Robbie or Uncle Brodie. Jamie is a Scot, not a Norseman."

Jake scowled just as the keep's main door slammed opened against the stone wall. A man stood there, looking around the hall.

"Uncle Logan!" Jamie cried. Though not a true uncle, Logan and Micheil Ramsay had been considered close relations ever since Alex's sister Brenna married Quade Ramsay, their brother.

Jake mirrored the greeting with his own yell, and they were hugging him in a moment. Then out of Logan's pocket came a handful of nuts for their enjoyment. "Go on outside and see if you can crack them open."

They headed out the door, but Maddie called out, "Your mantles, lads!"

The two rushed back in, pushing each other out of the way just so one would arrive at his destination first, their usual competition, then donned their mantles, yelling in unison over their shoulders, "Many thanks, Uncle Logan."

Once they were gone, Logan stomped his feet on the floor to clear off any mud and snow he'd gathered along the way. A couple of inches of snow had fallen last eve, leaving a coating of white on everything, including the tree branches. "They keep you busy, do they not, Maddie?"

Maddie let out a big sigh. "Aye, they do. I don't know what I would do without Alice here to assist me. I'll be glad when Jennie returns from Ramsay Castle. She was always such a big help. You look half frozen. Winter has settled in." Alex's youngest sister, Jennie, spent her time between the two castles of her eldest brother and her only sister, Brenna.

Logan glanced around and declared, "Aye, 'tis a cold one out there. 'Tis good you have the bairn dressed warmly, and yourself." He placed a packaged wrapped in twine on the table. "Gwynie sent more leggings for you and the lass to wear under your gown."

Maddie set Kyla down and reached for the package. "Many thanks to Gwyneth. I love her leggings and so does Kyla, but she grows so quickly." She opened the gift and swooped her daughter into her arms, swiftly pulling the new, soft leggings up to her waist to keep her bottom warm. The lass wiggled to get away from her mother, then grabbed Maddie's woolen gown as she set her feet on the floor and scanned the area, probably looking for her now absent brothers.

Kyla, apparently satisfied that her brothers were gone, toddled away from her mother, straight toward the wooden swords.

"Nay, lassie. You don't need to fight." The lassie was always imitating her brothers.

Kyla scowled and gave her mother a look that said she didn't agree. Maddie held back a grin and handed her daughter a fabric puppy to play with. The wee lassie tucked the soft toy against her, but Maddie knew she would reach for the sword as soon as her back was turned.

Logan said, "She's walking already. Did she not just turn a year?"

"Aye, a few moons ago." Maddie glanced back at Kyla, who managed to grab a sword, as predicted.

"She's feisty like her sire," Logan added, chuckling, taking the wooden weapon away from Kyla before Maddie could. "You want the sword, do you not, lassie?"

Kyla grinned up at Logan, smiling widely to show off her new teeth, her nearly black hair a sharp contrast to her bright smile. Since her hair was dark like her sire's, the older she got, the more she looked like a female replica of Alex.

Maddie let out a deep sigh. "Aye, all three are feisty. Mayhap our next one will be the quiet one." She moved away from the door and toward the hearth, lifting Kyla up and setting her down in the warmer area of the hall, not far from the sideboard so she could take care of her guest.

Logan snorted in response. "Not sure you'll ever see a quiet one."

Maddie stepped over to the sideboard and filled a goblet of ale. She then asked a passing serving lass for a tray of cheese and fruit before turning back to her guest. "Please sit down, Logan. What brings you here? Alex should be here from the lists any moment."

Logan sat with a huff, sweeping his long hair back with one gesture, and said, "I come bearing an invitation. Brenna attributes her love of Christmas and Yule to you, Maddie. Said you brought your own traditions from England. As Bethia is less than a year, Brenna's not interested in traveling again yet. They were just here because of the big battle, so she would like you all to join us at Ramsay Castle for the holiday. I hope you'll come. My Gwynie thinks she may be carrying."

"Oh, what news! Are you looking forward to a new bairn of your own?"

"Of course I am. And since I cannot keep my

hands off my wife's lovely arse, I am not verra surprised. A wee lassie, I hope." He smiled. "But truly, we might have considered coming here since Brenna wishes to have all the Grant siblings together, but with Bethia, Molly, and Maggie, we wouldn't dare travel. 'Tis too soon for our adopted lasses. Molly and Maggie are afraid to leave Ramsay land. Said they're afraid Randall Baines will find them. I can't do it to them. 'Tis why I came without Gwynie."

Logan and Gwyneth had adopted two lasses who'd been sold by their parents to a cruel nobleman. Maddie's heart tugged for the girls.

"I understand. If we came—and I would love to—I don't know if Ashlyn and Gracie could leave." Ashlyn and Gracie had been through a trauma not long ago. A cruel man who had controlled their mother had chased them and their mother, Caralyn, all the way to the Highlands from a small village on the coastline of Ayr, where he'd forced them to live. Caralyn had recently married one of Alex's brothers, Robbie, who had helped her escape the fool and taken in her two daughters, vowing to raise them as his own. "The girls have their own fears, but so does Caralyn. I believe Robbie and his family would remain here. Even so, I hope Alex will agree to it—I'm sure he would."

The door opened as if on cue, and Alex filled the doorway, stomping his boots just outside the door. "What will Alex agree to do?"

"Travel to Ramsay Castle for Christmas," Logan said. "You're all invited. You, Brodie, Robbie, and your families. Maddie tells me Robbie would stay here. Even so, with Jennie already with Brenna, you will nearly all be together." He glanced at the large man filling the doorway, also chieftain of the clan. "Brenna's fixing to make room for all of you while I'm gone. She's already set Quade to building all kinds of furniture. But my brother would do anything for his new wife, as you know. He adores Brenna. Mayhap he'll be adding a tower or two by the time I return."

Alex removed his mantle, placing it on the peg by the door and grabbed an ale from the sideboard. "As enticing as that sounds, the Norse presence remains heavy in the Highlands, and they search for travelers to take their anger out on. I don't suspect we'll be going anywhere with the bairns for at least another year."

"Year?" Maddie asked, stopping the organizing she was doing in the hall. She had moved away to begin preparations for their departure during Logan's explanation, believing they'd likely set off tomorrow. Alex's words shocked her. "Not for a year? Surely you do not mean that, Alex. A year is a verra long time."

Logan snorted in agreement. "I understand your concern, Grant, but 'tis the holiday, and if I don't bring you back, I'll have to answer to that new ornery mistress of my castle."

Alex set his goblet down and settled his hands on his hips. "Would that ornery mistress you refer to be my sister?"

Logan chuckled. "You know I jest. She's verra dear to me, but 'struth is there are others asking."

"Who?" Maddie asked, sitting in a chair near the hearth, handing a toy to Kyla, who ignored her and waddled over to her father.

"Upsy?" She stared up at him, her hands waving in the air over her head.

Alex leaned down to pick up his daughter, kissed her cheek, and said, "I'm sure I can guess. The only two Logan cannot refuse."

Maddie gave her husband a perplexed look.

"Wise arse," Logan replied.

"'Ise arse," Kyla mimicked.

"Logan!"

"Mayhap she may not—"

"'Ise arse!" Kyla grinned at Maddie's groan, wrinkling her nose as she giggled.

Logan looked chagrined and said, "Sorry, Maddie." Then he took Kyla away from her father and swung her high into the air. "You wee trickster. You got me in trouble."

Kyla giggled with glee, and as soon as he set her back down, Kyla looked at him and said, "'Ise arse."

Alex barked, "Kyla, you'll not be talking like a reiver."

He picked her up and set her on his shoulders, one of her favorite places to be. Then he spun in a few circles, Kyla weaving back and forth in the air a bit as he moved. She laughed louder and louder, hanging onto her father's long dark locks.

Maddie said, "Alex, be careful."

Alex shot her a grin but dutifully set Kyla down before settling himself into a chair in front of the fire.

As soon as the wee one's feet hit the floor, she took off toward the spot in the corner where her father kept his extra swords. Though the swords were well-protected from the bairns inside a wooden case it was still their favorite place to go, their wee fingers trying to reach through the narrow space between the slats. "Alex, I fear someday she'll manage to reach inside there. You must find a better place to keep your weaponry, a place none of them can reach."

"Maddie, they just need to learn not to touch them. 'Tis no' a difficult concept to teach them."

"Since 'tis not difficult, then I'll settle this task on your shoulders, Alex. Please teach the bairns not to try to take your weapons all the time."

Alex gave a low grumble as he chased after Kyla. "You wee troublemaker. Now I'm in trouble because of you." He swung her back into the air, her feet flying over Alex's head, and she carried on with such delight that everyone in the hall stopped to watch the interplay between the large Highlander and his wee daughter.

Maddie drawled, "I do not think that will work, Alex. And I have too much on my hands to watch over her all the time. Please take it seriously."

Logan said, "I'm guessing 'tis time for you and Maddie to get some of those herbs from your sister. The ones that postpone another bairn's arrival for a time."

Alex smirked, then glanced at Maddie, who felt herself turn hot with embarrassment. "'Tis too late for that. Our fourth could be on the way. One never knows." He grabbed the fabric puppy and sat in a chair, placing Kyla on his lap, who eagerly took the stuffed toy to play with.

"You could not keep your hands to yourself, Grant? Give your wife a reprieve?"

"I don't think my wife would be pleased if I chose to do that, Logan. Do you give your wife any rest?"

Maddie abruptly stood up and cleared her throat. "If you do not change your conversation, I'll throttle one of you. 'Tis not appropriate for a wee one to hear. She picks up on everything you men say." Though she wished she could rid herself of the redness on her cheeks, blushing was a trait that never left her. "Alex, I'd prefer to discuss our visit to your newest niece. And who are the two you cannot refuse, Logan?"

Alex replied for him. "Torrian and Lily, if I were to guess. He doesn't care about Brenna."

Logan snorted. "Aye, you've the right of it. That wee lassie with the golden hair knows just how to beg. She wants 'Unca Alex.' You know how fond Lily is of you. You, too, Maddie. Of course."

Maddie laughed. "I know his appeal more than anyone, Logan. And Lily is a smart lassie. We should go, Alex. It will not take me long to pack. We can be ready by the morrow."

"Nay, we'll not go. I'm sorry to disappoint Lily and Brenna, but I'll not risk it."

Kyla grew tired of sitting still, hopped off her sire's lap, and took off at a wobbly run toward the door.

"Alex," Maddie said, while chasing Kyla to the door, afraid someone would open it and hit the little lassie. "How many guards do you have? I think we have enough to protect our three bairns on a journey to Ramsay land. It would be lovely to have us all together again, to meet the holiday surrounded by family."

She snatched up Kyla and set her down again in the opposite direction, where Logan waited with open arms. Encouraged, Kyla ran over to him.

Alex stood up then, moved over to his wife, and wrapped his arms around her. He nuzzled her neck and whispered, "My apologies, sweeting, but I cannot allow it. Mayhap this summer, when the weather is fine." He kissed her cheek and then went to open the door in response to a sudden pounding.

He swung it open and the lads shoved right past him, already chattering. "Papa, where is Uncle Logan? We need more nuts."

"They were delicious, and we cracked them with the biggest rocks we could find," Jake said, swinging an imaginary boulder over his head and onto the ground.

"'Twas easy except for the last one," Jamie said, making his way over to Logan. "Do you have more, Uncle Logan?"

"Why did you come, Uncle?" Jake asked, stopping in front of his chair and looking up at him.

Maddie regarded the trail of mud following the lads and sighed. "Lads, look at the mess you've brought in. Go back to the door and take your boots off, please."

Logan ignored the lads to look at their father. "Alex, please reconsider the journey."

"A journey? May I come?" Jamie asked, as he returned to the door to belatedly remove his boots.

"And me," Jake practically shouted. "Where are we going?"

"Nowhere, lads. Do as your mother says and remove your boots and mantles."

"Is the journey on the morrow?"

"How long is the journey?"

"May we ride our own horses?"

"Does Kyla have to come?"

"Can we sleep under the stars, Papa?"

The two lads continued peppering their father with questions, but Alex just turned to Logan. "Many thanks to you, Logan. Now you've made me the bad one to my bairns, as well. You may stay the night, and then I ask you to return to your keep before you cause more trouble."

Logan guffawed, slapped his knee, and said, "With pleasure, Grant."

Alex headed into the kitchen and the lads chased him, leaving Logan and Maddie alone for a moment.

Maddie whispered, "I'll convince him."

Logan said, "I'm not sure about that, Maddie. He seems pretty set in his ways. I don't know if you've ever noticed it or not, but Alex is a wee bit stubborn."

Maddie's jaw inched up a bit and she whispered, "So am I. You can count on me being there with the bairns, with or without him."

Logan arched a brow at her and opened his mouth to reply, but Alex came back in with a half loaf of bread, and he wisely fell silent.

CHAPTER TWO

ALEX KNEW IT would *not* be one of their better nights. The firm set of Maddie's shoulders when she entered their chamber told him more than he needed to know.

"Maddie…"

She approached him, standing an arm's length away. "Alex, may we please talk about this?" Even that slowing of her step didn't bode well for her mood. She usually came as close as she could to him, and his favorite part was when she leaned into him, especially when he could take in her scent.

Apparently, he'd have to make the first move this eve.

"Aye, I'll listen," he said, closing the distance between them. His hands began their familiar path across her luscious body, caressing her curves exactly how and where she enjoyed it most. Unable to stop himself, he pulled her into a full embrace, glad to see she allowed it. How he loved the feel of her softness against him, her sweet lavender scent taking away all the odiferous smells of fighting warriors after a day in the lists.

Her chin jutted out. "Your soft touches feel verra nice, but I know your intent. You mean to distract me, to make me forget everything with your lovemaking. I'll not have it yet, husband."

He smiled, though cursing himself for not being able to slow his desire for her, giving his intent away as clearly as if he'd put words to his thoughts. He'd accommodate her wish, using a more subtle tactic. "Lie next to me. I am allowed to cuddle you while I listen, am I not? Tell me your thoughts, then."

"Verra well." She settled herself in her favorite position, lying on her side tucked in next to him with her head resting on his shoulder. "I thought long about this as I checked Logan's chamber and settled the bairns for the night. We should be able to visit your sister. Is this not why you train your warriors so hard? Is it not why you have worked so diligently to build your numbers? You have so many men. I'm sure you have enough to protect us from a few stray Norsemen."

Hellfire, but the woman always posed logical arguments.

He wrapped his arm around her, settling his hand on the sweet curve of her bottom and rubbing light circles there, something he knew slowly built her passion. "Aye, but I also must leave a force back to protect Grant Castle, unless you'd prefer to come home to find it taken over by others. And 'twill be a tough travel, Maddie, no matter how many I bring with us."

"I miss Brenna and I would so love to see wee

Bethia again. I cannot wait to see Kyla and her together. They're nearly the same exact age. And think how much fun the twins will have playing with Torrian and Lily. Lily will pretend to be a wee mama to both Bethia and Kyla. Do you not want to see that, Alex?"

"I would, Maddie. Yet you know I never make rash decisions, sweeting, especially when it comes to the ones closest to my heart. Will you allow me a day or two more to consider it? I'd like to send a patrol out and speak with Robbie and Brodie about this situation."

Her bottom wriggled, the first sign that his tender ministrations were working. She gave him her answer with a husky breath, making him smile.

"Aye, two days, no more."

"Agreed."

He then rolled them in one smooth motion, leaning over Maddie with a groan. His lips descended on hers, his weight on his elbows; then he lifted himself enough to peel off her night rail in one smooth motion, only breaking their kiss for a moment. His hand found her breast and caressed it until he heard her sweet whimpers in his ear. Her passion prompted him to take her nipple in his mouth, teasing her with his tongue before raking his teeth across the sensitive peak.

Her nails responded immediately, digging into his shoulder as she whispered, "Alex, please be quick about it, and do not torture me the way you like to."

"Ah, Maddie, but I do love you so." He settled between her thighs just the way he liked and plunged inside her with one thrust, unable to hide his own groan of pleasure when he seated himself deep inside her. He made a point of holding himself still for that one special moment—doing so always managed to squeeze out that extra bit of pleasure once he finally climaxed. He nuzzled her neck, savoring this short moment they shared before they began their dance, then paced his thrusts until she caught up with him, matching her pulses to his.

"Harder!" Her one-word command drove him nearly over the edge. He loved nothing more than hearing his sweet wife voice her demands.

Grinning like a laddie in the stables, he asked, "You wish to finish quickly, love?"

"Aye," she ground out between her clenched teeth, her tension visible in the lines of her jaw. He could tell how close she was just by her words.

He knew exactly how to push her over the edge, touching her in just the right spot or two. "My pleasure," he groaned. A moment later, he whispered, "Rather, your pleasure." Her final gasps nearly finished him, but it was the rhythmic contractions of her insides that sent him over the edge.

He'd barely managed to roll onto his back, bringing Maddie with him, before his dear wife fell asleep in his arms, a smile on her face.

The following morn, the bedchamber door flew open, and the twins bounded inside, climbing up onto the large bed.

"Mama, Papa," the dark-haired Jake said, his voice so full of excitement that Maddie immediately knew it had been precipitated by Logan Ramsay.

"What is it, lads?" Alex asked, climbing out of bed and donning his tunic and plaid.

Jamie, his blond curls a mess, looked up at his sire quite seriously. "Papa, do you not get cold sleeping with naught on?"

"Nay. Finish what you came to say, Jake." Alex was deft at redirecting the attention of the lads.

"Uncle Logan wishes to take us sliding down the small hill. He checked last eve and said there's enough snow on that hill, and he found a contraption at the carpenter's that we could use. Said he told the carpenter how to perfect it and that it would be ready this morn. Can we try? Please?"

Jamie added, "He's done it on Ramsay land with Torrian and Lily. He promises we'll not be hurt. He said he'll keep a keen eye on us."

Alex looked at Maddie for an answer, but Maddie had no idea what the contraption would look like or what the dangers of such a thing could be. "Alex, I'm not sure."

"Let us see what Logan intends," Alex said. Then, turning to the boys, he said, "Go ahead, but you must wear your trews and tunics and woolen socks. No plaid, or you might catch on a tree. We'll be out to check on you in a few moments."

The two boys hooted and raced out the door. "Are you sure it will be safe?" Maddie asked, worrying over everything that was initiated by Logan. "You know how he can be," she whispered, as if he would hear their discussion through the walls.

"'Tis exactly why I told them trews and tunics. I don't trust his plans, but I do trust our carpenter. I'll make sure our laddies are safe. I've heard of other contraptions that are quite entertaining." He leaned over the bed and lifted her up, giving her a quick cuddle. "I have sweet memories, lass of mine."

"Alex, I'm far from a lass." She tugged at her night rail in a sad effort to keep it in place, having donned it a short time ago.

"You'll always be my lass, forever." He kissed her soundly on the mouth and gave her a playful bounce by dropping her back onto the bed. She laughed but rearranged her night rail, then climbed out of bed and headed to the door. "You could stay and we could try it again." His grin told her exactly what he meant.

"And trust that Logan will take care of the lads?" she asked, her hands on her hips.

"You win. I'll hurry along."

Once Alex finished dressing, Maddie opened the door, not surprised to see her maid, Alice, headed her way.

"What has them so excited this morn?" Alice asked, looking from Maddie's face to Alex's. "I probably need not ask, as I am sure it would be the fine Logan Ramsay."

"Aye, he's going to show them how to slide down the snowy hill in some contraption. Would you get Kyla up and dress her, please? We're going out to check on Logan, and we'll take her along."

"The babes have all broken their fast, so all's left

is the dressing. I'll see to Kyla, my dear. And I do believe the sky is gray, so the snow will not melt so quickly. A good day for it."

Maddie smiled as the maid turned to fetch Kyla. Alice had been Maddie's maid for most of her life and came with her from England, and she adored the bairns. The truth was Maddie would be lost without her. She'd married their stablemaster before Maddie had met Alex, and she'd never been happier. Mac could always put a smile on Alice's face.

Alex finished his ablutions, came over, and kissed Maddie's cheek. "I'll leave you to dress while I go in search of food. May I bring you anything?"

"Nay, I'll hurry along so we can make certain both lads do not decorate the snow with blood."

"Aye." He chuckled.

"And don't forget your promise, Alex."

He stopped and turned back to her. "Promise?"

She sighed and said, "To consider our Yuletide journey."

"Aye, I'll speak with my brothers later."

He left and she finished her ablutions, then dressed with the cold weather in mind. The last thing she did before heading downstairs was brush her long blonde locks and plait them. On her arrival, the hall was full of boisterous chatter. The boys stood next to their uncle, waiting for him to finish his porridge and warm cup of broth.

"Good morn to all," she said.

"Mama, I have my boots and trews on, ready to

go," said Jamie, his eyes bright.

Jake added, "I'm ready to go whenever Uncle Logan is ready."

"Lads, I'm glad you're prepared." She bent down and planted a kiss on the top of each head. "Why don't you leave your uncle for a moment and play by the fire? I'd like you to keep an eye on your sister while I chat with him. Where is Papa?"

"He went to the lists already," Logan answered. "He said he'd be back in a quarter hour. He took an entire loaf of bread with him."

She glanced over at the hearth as Jake said, "Come, Kyla. We'll play swords."

They pulled out their small wooden swords, handing Kyla the smallest.

Kyla shook her head and said, "Nay!"

"Here, Kyla. This one is for you," Jake tried again.

"Big! Big!" Kayla shouted, pointing at the larger wooden swords.

"Mama!" Jake said.

"Lads, the longer it takes me to talk to Uncle Logan, the longer it will be before we can leave."

Jamie said, "Just give her what she wants, Jake. I want to go outside."

"Big! Shakey. Big!"

Jake handed over the larger sword, which dwarfed the small girl, but she happily sat on the ground to play with it.

Her children settled, Maddie looked back to Logan.

He arched his brow at her. "You wish to speak

with me?"

She lowered her voice so as not to capture the children's attention. "Aye. And I'll have your word you'll not tell Alex."

"If you say so, but what do you wish to keep from your husband?" He took a sip of broth and set his mug down, his eyes locked on hers.

"I'm going to Ramsay land."

"Ah," Logan said, relief tingeing the word. "Aye, I think he'll come around to the idea. He needs to think on it a bit, let it simmer inside."

"I know my husband. He has made his mind up already and is thinking on it just to placate me. If he refuses, I'm coming without him. I'll be a day behind you, and I'll bring the bairns, along with Alice and Mac. If I cannot catch up with you, I'll stop at one of our allies and ask for an escort of ten warriors. But I'm hoping you'll wait to see if I'm along. Alex will send an army along once he learns of it, so I'm not worried. He'll be behind us within half a day. I'm not putting us at risk."

"Maddie, let him think on—"

"Aye, I've asked him to consider it. Have tried asking politely and given him multiple logical reasons. But there are times where my husband is unreasonable." She cast an eye around the hall, making sure no one could overhear their whispered conversation. "I promise you I'm going whether he wishes to or not. I'm warning you in case I don't get the chance to speak with you later about this."

"Maddie, what you ask is too much. I cannot do that to Alex. He'll string me up by my bollocks." His face told her he was indeed worried about the possibility.

"It might be worse if he finds out I told you and you didn't wait for us, and we do this on our own. You can say you found us along the way and had to protect us."

The door opened and Alex stepped inside, big as life, so she ended the conversation, put on a bright smile, and was grateful for the lads who all headed Alex's way with a shout.

"Don't forget, Logan," she warned.

Because she was going whether Logan and Alex agreed or not.

CHAPTER THREE

ALEX TRUDGED OUT to the lists, where he knew he would find his two brothers. He thought it prudent to appear to sincerely contemplate this journey, or his wife would not be happy with him. He had to make her believe he was giving the invitation due consideration, even if he was not in truth, because Maddie could be a fierce one when she wanted to be.

He did not understand her insistence. How could she expect him to risk the lives of the five of them as well as the men and servants they'd bring along? Three bairns would be difficult to keep content in the middle of winter in the cold of the Highlands; the wind would blow until their cheeks were red, and their noses would run through the whole trip. The boys would probably consider it an adventure. In fact, he could tell them they were to protect their sister from reivers, and they'd take that job seriously, keeping their attention on the landscape for the duration of the journey.

And what of the other, more menacing dangers? Maddie couldn't comprehend how it felt to be on the battlefield with the Norse and their bludgeoning hammers, which were able to split a skull in two without much effort. The Norse were ruthless.

That was something his brother Robbie knew. He'd saved Caralyn from a life as a prostitute on a galley ship. She'd been moments away from being dragged on board the ship by a tall Norseman who had enjoyed beating her first when Robbie had rescued her.

Yet he knew his wife. Maddie had determined they'd go, and she was as difficult to convince to give up her quest as he. Perhaps it would be prudent to truly give consideration to her idea and how it could be managed. Aye, that would give him even more substance to help explain how difficult this journey could be. But he also had to give in to the thought he didn't wish to consider. He could possibly decide to let his wife have her wish granted. So he forced himself to think on the possibilities. Just in case it was he who changed his mind.

Alex would have to find some way to protect Maddie and the wee ones from the elements. The carpenter could craft a new cart for the journey. He could conceivably build two sides up so they could cover it with furs if it snowed.

If they traveled with Alice and Mac, Maddie would have assistance. Brodie's wife, Celestina, would surely go with them which would be more help with the bairns. But he had to think on how many guards to take along and how many to leave behind. This he would discuss with his brothers if he decided to go.

Arriving at the stables, Alex found Robbie chatting with Mac, the stable master, and Brodie. He approached his youngest brother. "Brodie, I thought you would be sliding or rolling down the hill with the lads by now."

Brodie replied, "Rolling is fun, but I'm anxious to see this contraption Logan has had the carpenter create."

"I am too. I'll be there so my lads don't get killed by a wild uncle."

Brodie, Mac, and Robbie all chuckled. Alex just arched a brow, wondering why the possibility of his lads getting hurt would entertain them.

"Also, I'd like to know what you all have heard from patrols about Norsemen in the area."

"Why? Is there a new threat?" Robbie asked.

"The threat is Maddie. Or mayhap Logan. It depends how you wish to see the situation. Logan brought the message that Brenna invites us all to Ramsay Castle for Christmas."

All three nodded their heads, waiting to see what Alex would say. When he said nothing, Robbie finally spoke.

"I'll volunteer to stay and protect the castle. Ashlyn and Gracie say they're never leaving Grant land again. I wouldn't put them through it just yet. Mayhap when they're a wee bit older and trust that I'm not going to give them back."

"Give them back?" Brodie asked.

"I heard Ashlyn speaking with Gracie. The lass told her sister that if they were still here at

Christmas, then I probably wouldn't be giving them back to the bad man. Caralyn can't quite convince them I'd never do such a thing. Time will prove it."

"But if you stay, Robbie, then you'd be here alone while we all went to Ramsay land. We've always tried to spend Christmas together," Brodie countered.

"We won't be all together in any event. Even if we all stay here, both Brenna and Jennie are on Ramsay land. Jennie will be upset if the rest of you don't go." Life had been mostly calm in the Highlands, but the war with the Norse had changed much for their family. Now four of them had spouses, so Jennie, the youngest, split her time between the two clans. "My family are looking forward to their first Christmas in the Highlands. Nicol and Inga will be here, and others. We'll be far from alone." Robbie gave a convincing argument. Nicol was Brodie's best friend and assistant throughout the war and had married Celestina's maid not long ago.

Alex nodded. "Before I make my final decision, I'd like to know what your patrols have found over the past week. And what are they hearing from our neighbors? Any trouble? Any reivers foolish enough to come this far north of the borders to try to steal cattle?"

Robbie scratched his head. "We have not seen many Norse. No reports that I'm aware of. They're probably closer to the firths so they can jump back in their galley ships quickly if the weather takes a turn for the worse."

"But we did catch signs of reivers in the area. 'Twas a sennight ago. Naught since."

Alex ran his hand along his jaw. "Then there remain some threats out there. Send another patrol out with a focus on reivers or wandering Norsemen or anyone in the area who doesn't belong. I want a full report this eve."

"Aye, Chief." As second-in-command to the laird of Clan Grant, it was Robbie's job to see that Alex's instructions were followed. "There is always some kind of threat in the Highlands. You know that, Alex. But you have plenty of warriors to protect them all. What say you? What did you say to your wife?"

Alex rubbed his hands together to warm them up, then turned away to pace in a small circle. He knew his brother's words to be true. There would always be danger, and he had a great many men. Yet no matter how he tried, he couldn't rid himself of the vision of reivers closing in from all sides, attacking his wife and his beloved bairns, while he was unable to defend against their numbers.

"I made no promises yet," he finally said. "At first I said nay because I'm worried about the number of Norse still looking for revenge after the Battle of Largs. I told her we'd go next year."

"And?" Brodie leaned forward, the question had them all waiting for his answer.

"She asked me to think on it. I said I would, but I am of a mind to still deny her. She'll accept it in time. I know she'll be disappointed, but Maddie trusts my instincts."

Mac snorted. Brodie grinned. Robbie hung his head.

"Do you have something to say, Mac?" Alex bit out.

Though his anger flared, he'd trusted Mac's opinion on courting Maddie on multiple occasions, and he was loath to admit that the man had always been right. His brothers hadn't always known, but Mac knew exactly how Maddie's mind worked.

Mac took a step back. "Now don't be getting upset with me, Chief, but you know I'm an honest man, and I've been on this world a bit longer than you have, and I have a wee bit more experience with the female mind, particularly with your wife's."

"Aye, you've known Maddie many years. What of it?" Alex set his hands on his hips.

"Well, I know your lovely wife to be a stubborn woman, and she will not give the idea up easily if it's truly what she wants for Christmas." When Alex narrowed his eyes, Mac quickly added, "But I'm certain you can convince her."

"And you two? What say you?"

Brodie glanced over at Robbie before he spoke. "Maddie can be persistent."

"Aye, 'tis a good word," Robbie said. "I'd just give in to the lass now if I were you, Alex. It will make your life much simpler, aye? She'll wear you down. She usually does."

Robbie arched a brow at him as if challenging Alex to deny his beliefs about his and Maddie's marriage.

Alex couldn't believe his ears. Maddie always did what he said to do.

She loved him, trusted him. She would do what she was told as a good wife should. He did his best to discuss things with her, and he allowed her to speak her opinion inside their bedchamber, but when it came to battle and warriors, she would never question his decision.

What were Mac and his brothers talking about?

He felt they'd set a bit of a challenge to him. He'd be glad to prove them wrong.

Maddie picked up Kyla and made her way out to the hill, hoping she'd miss Alex. She needed to step away out of his sight to guarantee that her plan would be safe for her and the bairns.

Luck was on her side.

She wasn't surprised to see Ashlyn and Gracie already at the bottom of the hill. The first thing they did was fuss over Kyla, so Maddie set her down in the snow in her leather boots, smiling at her bulky appearance. Alice had bundled her in several thick furs, and she looked round, like a wee snowman. Kyla didn't seem to mind.

Of course, Kyla had broken into a smile on seeing the two lasses. "Shwee, Wacie. Pway."

Maddie knew Kyla was more advanced than most children her age. She spoke many words that the lads hadn't mastered until nearly their second year. Alice said it was because lasses were such talkers. But Maddie was certain it was because Kyla would prove to be an extremely bright and clever woman when she grew up. She would prove to be a gentle lady, just like her mother. Maddie smiled and bussed Kyla's cheek before releasing her into the care of her cousins.

Then she set off to her task. Logan could be leaving as soon as the morrow, so she needed to plan her trip carefully. If she had to leave on her own, she would need two others to travel with her since they'd have to ride three horses, one adult rider and one bairn per horse. Her most logical and first choice would be Mac and Alice.

She didn't think they'd have any trouble on the first day because Grant land was so deep into the Highlands. Alex kept speaking of reivers, but everyone knew they moved out in the cold of winter and headed back to the Lowlands. Besides, anyone in the area, including reivers, would be afraid of the powerful warriors of Clan Grant. Most who hoped to steal stayed far away from Grant land. Maddie's party would be off Grant land in a couple of hours, then would head south. If Logan chose to wait for her, then they'd have the protection of the Ramsay warriors for the rest of the journey.

And, of course, she also predicted that half a day after they left, Alex would be directly behind them, raging mad. She'd worry about his temper later—what mattered was that he'd come with warriors to chase after them. And, if she had her way, they'd be closer to Ramsay land than Grant land by then, so the safest plan would be to head to Clan Ramsay.

If he didn't speak to her for the entire time they

were there, she'd have many others to chat with, and the two of them would make up eventually. His anger would soften as soon as he saw his two sisters.

Besides, she'd learned soon enough in their marriage that if she got Alex alone and dropped her gown, shift, and plaid to the floor, he would do nearly anything she asked. True, it hadn't worked last eve, but he'd yet to refuse her completely.

She rounded a corner in the stables and nearly ran into Mac.

"Oh, your pardon, Mac. I was too preoccupied with my thoughts."

She smiled, trying to gauge Mac's mood.

At first he gave her a wide smile, his usual, but then his eyes narrowed. "What have you planned, young lady?"

She nearly snorted, not all that shocked that he knew her so well. "Whatever do you mean, Mac? Can I not just come for a visit?"

"Out with your request."

She glanced over her shoulder to see if they were alone, then pulled him down the passageway to the end of the stalls. "I'm asking a favor. You will be the only one who knows, so if he finds out, I'll know you're the one who betrayed me. And I'll never forgive you."

"I don't like the sound of this at all." His usual jovial demeanor changed quickly to a serious tone.

"I know not when we will be interrupted, so listen carefully. Logan invited us to spend Christmas with the Ramsays. Alex denied him. I've asked Alex to reconsider, and he is thinking on it, but I know my husband. He's just delaying his denial, searching for another good reason not to go."

"Ah, is this a request to argue your case? Gathering allies, Maddie? I'll see if I can reason with him. 'Tis not a difficult task at all, not with the number of warriors he has at his disposal. There would be more than enough to take with him and leave some behind."

"'Tis not what I'm asking."

Mac sent her a look of confusion. "What are you asking, then?"

"Alex will not be reasoned with when he is determined to deny a request. I have given him the sound reasoning, but I'll wait and see how he will reply. I'm waiting for him to admit to me that he'll not allow us to go."

"Then . . ." Mac trailed off, clearly uncertain what to say to that.

"I am here because once Logan leaves, I will follow him. I hope to catch up with him before Alex finds out and follows."

Mac's face was the picture of shock. "Maddie, with all due respect, you are not thinking this through carefully. You cannot do that. He'll be furious."

"I'll not be dissuaded, Mac. I only tell you as I want you to go with us. You and Alice. I cannot take three bairns safely on my own, so I need assistance. You are the only two I trust to keep your word. And if you tell Alex, neither I nor your wife will forgive you. What say you?"

Mac found his tongue and finally said, "Maddie, why? Why would you anger your husband so and take such a risk?"

"Because there's no reason we cannot go safely. He's not listening to reason. I'll not be dictated to as I was with Kenneth." Mac should understand. He was there when the man she thought to be her brother had mistreated her, confined her to her chamber, refused to allow her to do anything without his approval. He was the worst form of dictator there could be.

While she knew in her heart that Alex was not like Kenneth, a small inkling warned her to be careful, to not allow another to control her as Kenneth had.

"Alex is not like that, Maddie. You know that well."

"I know that to be true," she said, tears dotting her lashes. "But you know better than anyone how I was controlled. I need him to see that he cannot do the same, Mac." A fire had started deep in her belly that wouldn't be easily extinguished. Her last statement came out in a whisper. "It was not that long ago and I have not forgotten any of it. Please."

Mac sighed heavily. "All right. I do not agree with this, Maddie, but I know you're a stubborn woman. I'll go along with you, but only until we meet up with Logan. For the safety of the bairns."

"'Tis all I need of you. That and three horses hidden in the forest just outside the gates when I give you notice. I know not exactly how this will play out, so we must be ready for any situation. Hide the animals in a place where they'll not be seen in the dark. Remember, I'll know if you tell Alex."

"He'll have me beaten when he learns I did not inform him," Mac replied.

"What Alice will do to you would be worse."

"Why won't you see reason, lass? Speak to Alex. Do not sneak off as you plan."

"I have spoken to him, Mac, but it's no use. You'll see that he intends to deny us." Maddie paused. "Alice will be going with me, whether you go or not. She gave my mother her word that she'd always watch over me. I thought your loyalty was to your wife. Or have you become more loyal to Alex? If so, I'll make sure Alice knows where she ranks in importance to you."

Mac paled. "Maddie, when did you gain this cruel streak?"

"It is not cruelty. It is determination." She spun on her heel before Mac could say more. When she was far enough away from him, she mumbled to herself, "It is determination and survival."

She was going to Ramsay land, and nothing was going to stand in her way.

Not even Alex Grant.

CHAPTER FOUR

ALEX REMOVED HIS mantle and hung it on the peg near the door, then stomped his boots, which Maddie strictly enforced. She had learned much from Brenna about maintaining the cleanliness of the keep for the bairns, and Brenna had learned it from their mother, also a renowned healer, so it was difficult for Alex not to go along with his wife on these matters. Of course, in many ways, she had also proven to mother differently when it came to their babes: nursing them all on her own, even the twins, and refusing to hang them on the wall in a binding as was tradition.

When Alex had questioned her about the latter, she'd said, "Would you like to be hung on the wall, Alex?"

"But they're bairns, Maddie, and they can see all that goes on from the wall."

It had worked for others—why not his bairns? But Maddie had not allowed it whenever a maid had mentioned such a practice.

"You may hang them on your chest for the

warmth, but that is all I will accept, Alex," she'd said. "They are sweet babes who deserve our best care."

Maddie had followed everything Brenna had suggested about changing the rushes often, keeping the dogs in one area of the hall, not allowing the men to throw bones on the floor, and bathing more often than anyone he knew. While Brenna and Alex's mother had started some of these ideas—she also didn't allow bones to be thrown on the floor—Brenna had taken that desire for cleanliness even further, and Maddie had adopted most of her practices. One odd one she'd started on her own was insisting on washing the bairns in a basin every day.

"But why, Maddie?" he'd asked.

"Would you like to lie in your own urine every day?"

He'd not argued with her, giving in to her sensibilities because she'd been English when he married her. And though she was now Scottish, none of the things she'd insisted upon were any bother to him, so what did it matter?

It had been Mac who had convinced him of that simple truth, and it had proven to be great advice. He'd looked at Alex and said, "Do you care if she washes the bairns when you're not around?"

Alex had stared at the floor, thinking on Mac's simple wisdom and eventually shook his head. "Nay, I guess I don't."

Mac had chuckled, clasped his shoulder, and said, "You'll find plenty of reasons to argue with her. Let her do as she wishes."

Why, he'd even worked on a plan to give his wife a special bathing chamber above stairs. He and his brothers had concocted a contraption of ropes to draw water up in pails and allow it to heat in the sun before dropping it into tubs. He'd been surprised at how well the plan had worked.

And how appreciative his wee wife had been. That thought brought a smile to his face, but he lost it as quickly as it had come when he thought of how disappointed she'd be when they didn't travel to visit Brenna and Jennie.

Now, traveling to Ramsay land in the cold of winter with three bairns would be a bother. But he knew that reason would not be enough.

He sighed, dismissing the thought for the moment. The end of the day was upon them, and he looked forward to a quiet eve eating good food and chatting with Logan by the fire, with Maddie next to him.

He trudged across the hall just as Maddie entered from the kitchens, Kyla on her hip, as she often was.

"Pa . . . pa . . . pa . . . pa," the wee lassie called, her arms held out to him. His sweet daughter smiled, and he swept her up in his arms, tossing her overhead until she giggled.

"Alex, have you given my proposal any more thought?"

Hell, how he wished he could give her an answer she'd like. "Aye, Maddie, and I feel it is too risky. I'm sorry to disappoint you, but there are still Norsemen about, and with three bairns, I cannot risk travel at this time of the year. Mayhap in the warmer months of summer."

"Do you not plan to have more bairns, Alex?"

He didn't like her tone. He knew it to be the one of special reasoning, the kind he'd never be able to argue against. She was too quick by far when she wanted something.

His gaze narrowed and he answered, "You know I do." He settled Kyla on his shoulders, her preferred place to be. Her hands always managed to twirl the long strands of his hair into a mess, but it never stopped him from putting her in her favorite perch. "I'm confused by your question. Do you not wish for more bairns?"

"Of course I do. But if we continue to have bairns, we'll have even more little ones to travel with to Ramsay land. Perhaps we should go before we have another set of twins. Next year could be heavy with snow at the holiday, unlike this year. There are many reasons to go now while we can."

She stared up at him, her gaze hopeful, her hands folded neatly in front of her.

"Maddie, 'tis too dangerous—"

The door opened with a bang, and Logan entered with the twins directly behind him. Their laughter filled the space as they hung their mantles and left their boots at the door, full of mud, as they usually were.

"Look, Mama. Uncle Logan helped us climb the trees protected near the caves, where we found more apples. I have five and Jamie has four," Jake said, holding up his own bunch of apples. "And we found nuts, too."

Jamie stomped his foot. "Jake, I had five. You took one of mine. Give it back."

Kyla held her hand out over Alex's head and said, "Appo, pweez. Appo."

Brodie, Loki, and Robbie came in behind the two lads, Loki, Brodie's adopted son, carrying a sack of nuts. "We found lots of food for winter. I used my slinger to shoot the apples down. Look how many we have!"

Alex took Kyla over to the group, happy for an excuse to escape his conversation with Maddie. Loki offered Kyla a nut he had shelled and carried on. "'Twill be the best Yule ever. We'll have so much food and I cannot wait."

Logan moved over to the hearth, rubbing his hands together in front of the flames while Robbie tossed more logs into the fireplace and poked at the logs inside with an iron stick. "I'll not stay much longer. What have you decided, Grant?"

"Decided about what?" Loki shouted.

"About visiting Ramsay Castle for Christmas," Logan replied.

"I wish to go with Uncle Logan," Jake announced.

"Can we go with him, Papa. Please?" Jamie added.

"Nay, we cannot. Send our regrets to my sisters, Logan," Alex said. Logan frowned but nodded.

"We should go hunting one more time," Robbie added.

"I want pheasant for the Yule," Jake announced, starting off the twins' rapid-fire commentary.

Jamie shrugged. "Or a big goose."

"No, I want a big boar."

"And peas."

"Nay, fruit tarts."

"Uncle Logan, will you come back for Yule?"

Brodie, ignoring the twins, turned to Alex and asked, "How did Maddie take your rejection?"

"Was she upset?" Robbie added.

"Nay, she understands. I told you she would," Alex said with more confidence than he felt. He'd always believed Maddie agreed with his reasoning in nearly any issue they were confronted with, so he had no reason to think this situation would be any different . . . other than the firm tilt of her jaw and the narrowing of her eyes that told him she wasn't agreeable. Perhaps he'd better ask again.

"Is that not right, Maddie?" Alex turned around to get Maddie's confirmation, but she wasn't there. "Maddie?"

Where was she?

Brodie whispered, "Mayhap she's not as happy as you thought."

"She trusts my judgment. I'm sure she's just checking on the evening meal."

While Alex was distracted, Maddie took the opportunity to pack some food away for their journey. Moving into the kitchens, she found a hunk of cheese in the cupboard and several oatcakes. The apples the lads had found on an outing two days ago sat in a barrel close to the back door, so she sauntered over to the barrel and grabbed six for their trip.

No one questioned her, so she finished packing and set the sack in a hidden spot where no one would see it. Then she headed back into the great hall.

Alex made his way to her side immediately. "Were you seeking out Cook to discuss the evening meal?"

"Nay, Alex. I spoke with her earlier. I just like to check the stores occasionally and see what must be brought up from the cellars. It is just a usual task that many don't know that I do."

He grabbed her hand and tugged her back inside the kitchens. "Are we in need of anything? I can have barrels of ale brought in or sacks of oats. Just tell me your needs."

She patted his arm and said, "No need. We have plenty, so please do not worry. I have taken care of everything. May we finish our earlier discussion?"

"There is not much to say, Maddie. I told you I cannot risk my bairns' and my wife's life. I'm sorry if this displeases you, but it's my final decision. We'll stay here, as I've said."

His last words set her insides churning in fury and sent her back to the days when she lived with the man she'd falsely thought to be her half brother, Kenneth. She crossed her arms and stared up at her husband, doing her best to contain her rage. "So I am to stay imprisoned inside these walls as you bid me to do? You do recall the situation I was forced to live in before I met you?

Is that what my life will be like, Alex? Because I've lived that life before, and I was not happy."

The fire lit in her husband's eyes as quickly as her own fury had blossomed. She hated to bring it to this point, but she would not be a prisoner in her own home the same way she'd been with Kenneth.

"Do not dare compare me to the evil man whom you thought to be your brother. You insult me gravely by even the suggestion. There are times when I will have the final say, Maddie. And this is one of them." Each word rang out louder as he spoke it, his voice reaching a yell by the end. "Hear me, wife: We are not going to Ramsay land for the winter! And that is final!"

Alex spun on his heel and stormed out of the kitchens.

Maddie narrowed her eyes at his back. She did not like being caged, and she did not like being yelled at, either, especially in front of their servants and their bairns. She had told Alex as much, and yet here they were.

Memories of Kenneth and his overbearing ways filled her mind, causing her hands to shake. She would not give in to Alex, even though most days he was a reasonable and loving husband, the day she married him, she had vowed to herself that she would never lose her independence. She needed to impress upon him the importance of discussing and weighing his desire to protect with her need for freedom.

His yelling just made her decision easier.

She exited the kitchens and reentered the

great hall. Ignoring her husband, she hummed to herself while she tidied up and rethought her plan. She'd thought she'd wait for Logan, but Alex would be watching her too closely afterward now that he knew her true feelings. He'd be seeking ways to soften her disappointment and anger, and her chance at slipping away would be too reduced. No, she'd have to go ahead of Logan—now, tonight. If she remained, she feared another yelling session, and at that point, Mac or Alice might refuse to help her. She knew Logan had plans to leave early in the morn, at a time when the household would not yet notice her and the bairns' absence. He'd catch up to them within hours.

She hated to leave Alex on such a note, but he left her no choice. Losing his temper and yelling at her forced the issue, forced her to take action ahead of her plan.

Glad she'd already taken the time to pack fresh clothing for herself and the bairns, she began to adjust her list of tasks and preparations. Even as she did so, she felt a flash of further regret that Alex had not agreed to travel. If he had, then there would be a large cart or two going along with them, into which she could pack extra clothes and gifts for the Ramsays. Now she was limited. But it was not a deterrent. She knew Brenna would find clothing for all of them, when needed.

As the men filed outside in wait of the evening meal, she took advantage of the nearly empty great hall and made a point to inspect the lads' winter clothing, ensuring everything was in good repair. The lads, as usual, had chased the men without their mantles on, donning their short boots instead of the ones they wore in the snow. The cold rarely seemed to bother them, plus the meal was about to begin, so they'd return inside soon.

She found Celestina abovestairs and chatted with her for a wee bit while Alice took care of Kyla, then they both headed belowstairs as the men returned and the serving lasses brought out the trenchers of food. Sitting at the dais next to Alex, she was grateful for Logan's presence because the two chatted on about every issue the Scots had ever had, keeping her from having any conversation with her husband. She went over the checklist in her mind, making sure she would forget nothing.

She was ready.

After their evening meal, she turned to Alex. "Alex, I'm verra tired this eve. I'd like to go abovestairs with the bairns now. Please stay and keep Logan entertained." She leaned down to give him a kiss, then said, "Come along, lads." She swooped up Kyla, who let out a giggle, then took her up the staircase while the lads yelled their goodbyes to all.

Alice was inside the bairns' chamber, fussing about. "Evening all. I'm preparing everything as you've instructed, my dear."

Jake and Jamie ignored her as they hurried over to their corner of the chamber, where their weapons sat on a chest, just as the weapons did in their sire's chamber.

Maddie set Kyla down and approached Alice. With a whisper she said, "We go tonight."

"Have you a plan?"

"Aye, since I know his routine so well, I'll wait until he's sound asleep. Then I'll come to this chamber and we'll sneak out. The lads will sleep well after such a long day with Logan. And Kyla never awakens for any reason. They'll not move when we carry them outside."

"You've thought of everything. But why tonight?"

"Alex gave me his answer, and I know there is no changing his mind. I feel we must leave this eve while he is still distracted, or we may miss our opportunity. But Logan will be along shortly afterward. He is set to leave at first light, so we'll not get into trouble."

Alice nodded and said, "The Lord will watch over you because you have such a big heart, Maddie, and in turn keep us all safe."

How she prayed Alice was right.

CHAPTER FIVE

ALEX WAS SURPRISED to see his wife fast asleep when he entered their chamber. Their last words had not been pleasant ones, and he had expected a reconciliation on his arrival.

He sighed. While he regretted raising his voice, sometimes it was the only way Maddie would listen. Though, in truth, comparing him to that cruel bastard Kenneth had also set his temper off.

He looked at his wife. She looked beautiful lying on her side, the golden waves of her hair on the pillow behind her. He'd hoped that they'd complete the reconciliation as they usually did—in bed. Sometimes the best of their lovemaking occurred after such a reunion, but alas, it was not to be.

Remembering their lovemaking last eve would have to do. He couldn't stop the smile from crossing his face over his memories. Maddie was a passionate woman and wasn't afraid to show him. Of that, he was grateful.

Dropping his plaid on the floor, he climbed in behind his love and tucked her up against him, her deep sigh making him grin wider.

Lord, but he'd fallen hard for his sweet wife—more than he'd ever thought possible. Now if he could just convince her to trust his judgment in all decisions, their life would be much simpler and happier.

How could she find the idea of a trip through the Highlands with three bairns in the middle of winter the least bit enticing? As much as he would love to see Brenna and Jennie, too many questions plagued him: How could he be sure he'd keep them all warm? Or properly fed? Or protect them against boar and wolves and reivers?

He could envision Jake taking off into the woods to relieve himself and running straight into a boar who would drive its tusk straight . . .

Enough!

He clenched his jaw, willing the vision away.

Maddie had no idea how much responsibility it was to keep people safe in the wild lands of the Highlands. There were mudslides, avalanches, and heavy snow. There were reivers and Norsemen and enemies. It was not worth the risk.

He'd made the right decision. His wife would see that soon.

He closed his eyes, taking in Maddie's sweet scent, and fell fast asleep.

"This may work out better than I thought," Mac said as they made their way to the horses waiting for them in the field.

"Oh?" Maddie replied, surprised Mac would

say a good word about her plan.

"Aye. A storm's brewing, but we should be ahead of it. Once Logan awakens and senses it, he'll be right along behind us. And I'd rather see Logan coming than your husband, Maddie."

"Why?"

Mac shook his head. "Because once I see your husband coming, I'll be running the other way. He's going to kill me."

"You have oats, Mac?" Maddie asked, intentionally ignoring his comment. She held Jamie against her to keep him warm, Mac had Jake in front of him, while Alice had Kyla in a sling across her chest because she was the lightest of the three bairns.

"Of course. Now mount up. We need to leave quickly."

Alice had gotten their belongings and food sacks to Mac earlier, so he had them already attached to the horses' saddles. Maddie wore her heaviest mantle and thickest boots, warm woolen socks protecting her feet. The lads were covered in warm furs over their mantles. She'd even been able to dress them without awakening either one of them.

Logan had a way of tiring out even the wildest of bairns.

"Ready," she said, nodding to Mac, who'd just gotten Alice settled with Kyla, who was completely covered by her mantle, her dark hair sticking out underneath Alice's chin.

They traveled for half the night without event. The boys woke up, but they weren't the least bothered by the situation—though they had asked the questions she expected, beginning with Jake.

"Where are we? Where are we going?"

"Where's Papa? Why is he not with us?" Jamie added, looking around. "And where are the guards? Papa always sends guards with us."

"We're on a special adventure," Maddie explained. "'Tis your job to see Uncle Logan before he reaches us. Then Papa will come find us all after, but you must catch Uncle Logan first. 'Tis all part of the game."

"Aye," Mac said, following Maddie's cue. "You must keep watch for any reivers too. Or any boar."

"Aye, I'll hunt them down." Jamie swung a hand through the air like a sword, an evil edge to his voice.

"Brave lad," Maddie replied, patting his head as he sat in front of her.

A few hours later, Jake sat in front of Mac, eyes still searching for any attackers.

"If you see anyone, you let me know, lad."

"Aye, I'll slay them, Mac. I must protect my mother and my sister."

"And Alice," Mac added.

"Jamie will protect Alice."

Maddie guessed they had about four hours on the men. Logan would have left upon waking, and Alex would be shortly behind him. If he hadn't caught up with Logan already. "How many warriors do you think the lads will have to fight off, Mac?"

Mac glanced sideways at her with a heavy sigh,

apparently catching the true question behind the phony one. "I'll bet at least five score will come along eventually. Mayhap more."

That *should* have given Maddie a small sense of relief. After they were first married, she and Alex had come to an agreement that they would air their grievances only when alone. So the presence of Alex's men should postpone his chastising. But given how he'd raised his voice yesterday for all to hear, she now wasn't so sure an audience would spare her his immediate fury. Especially as Maddie knew her actions would push the limits of Alex's patience.

"Here comes the snow, Mama," Jamie said, tipping his head back with a wide grin, pointing at the big flakes floating through the air. The sky was one big mass of clouds, the moon peeking out just enough to light up their way. If it hadn't been a full moon, they probably wouldn't have been able to make the journey. The wind began to pick up, and the horses reacted right away, letting her know they didn't like the change in the weather.

Mac said, "Never mind them, Maddie. They'll keep going. We're well past Grant land now, however. So once we get through the narrow ravine, we should consider stopping in a cave."

"You think to stop?" Maddie asked. They'd not come all this way to stop too early and be dragged back to Grant land, yet she had to worry about everyone staying warm. Alice was not young anymore.

"Aye, I do. If we slow our travel, we'll be caught,

but I doubt they'll turn us back around from here. We must consider the safety of the bairns first. There is a large cave not far, one that can hold the horses under an outcropping. We'll need to keep our belongings dry, too. You'll not want anyone getting sick in the middle of a snowstorm."

Alice glanced over at Maddie and said, "My hands get so cold when the wind blows. I could use a warm fire soon."

Maddie looked at the sky; the snow was coming. She sighed. She'd have to trust they'd gone far enough. Logan would catch up with them here and escort them the rest of the way.

"Aye, Mac, the safety of all first. I agree. Let us get to this cave."

They reached the ravine and it was clear. The area was protected by rock ledges and outcroppings, so there was little snow to hamper their crossing. "We must get across before the snow starts to stick," Mac said.

"A great storm," Jake cried out. "Mayhap we'll have to build a cave in the snow." His eyes lit up at the possibility, and Maddie didn't wish to disappoint him.

His brother had no such qualms. "Jake, we'll be in a *real* cave. We must keep Alice warm."

Maddie led her horse across the ravine carefully, Mac in front of her and Alice behind her.

"Wait until we tell Papa," Jamie shrieked. "Jake, 'tis farther down than any place we've seen. We could roll down at the end."

"We could hide in the trees over there, catch the enemy unaware. It would be a great place to set a trap for the Norse." Jake said the word with an underlying hatred, rolling the end of it off his tongue with a bit of extra spittle. He then spit off to the side like a true Scot.

Maddie wasn't about to reprimand him on the ravine.

The Scots often had to fight the English over the years, but their most recent battle had been against the Norse and King Haakon, who wished to steal all the isles from the Scots. The clans had banded together and fought hard. Alex and his brothers all played a large part in the defeat of the Norse.

The lads were forever imitating their father and uncles, staging pretend battles and imaginary traps for the Norse.

They made it across the ravine without issue, and thankfully, it entertained the children more than Maddie had expected. Once on the other side, Mac slowed his horse, lifting his head to the wind before turning to her.

"Lead us to the cave, Mac."

Mac nodded in reply, a sober look on his face that she didn't fully understand. After all, if her husband could take the Grant band of warriors into the forest in any weather and survive, she didn't know why it would be difficult to survive in a cave.

Maddie worried more about Alice, though, who'd gone quiet. The bairns were strong and resilient, but she could see the toll the journey was taking on her dear maid. How long had it been since she'd been on horseback? In her younger days, Alice rode when she could, but not of late.

Maddie shook herself, releasing the worry. The men—whether Logan ahead of Alex or them together—couldn't be more than four hours behind them. There was nothing to be concerned about other than her husband's temper when he reached them.

CHAPTER SIX

"WHAT THE HELL do you mean she left?" Alex's roar could be heard across most of the Highlands, if he were to guess, though they were still in the great hall. He only hoped it reached Maddie's ears.

Logan said, "She's been gone for hours, is my guess. Are you going to stand here and holler or go after her?"

"Mayhap I should allow her to go alone. See how well she does." He paced in a circle. "And I'll kill Mac."

"I wouldn't do that. He went along to protect her, I'm sure. Would you rather he stayed back? You married a stubborn lass, Grant, and she was going one way or another. Her plan had been for me to leave and for her to follow if you did not come around. I did not argue, as I knew at least I could keep an eye on her that way. Why she decided to leave in the middle of the night, I don't know."

"You knew of her plan?" Alex snapped, his rage climbing.

Logan returned his stare without any fear. "I knew that nothing would stop a woman with that look in her eye. Telling you would have done nothing. And someone needed to be reasonable enough for her to trust him with her confidence. At least I know her plan—something you don't know. You yelled at her, not me."

Brodie came across the courtyard and held up a sack. "I've gathered enough food in case your wife forgot." He had a sack in his other hand. "Oh, and extra plaids. The storm will bring the winds up."

Robbie was directly behind Brodie, hiding his face from Alex. "And why are you hiding, Robbie? Are you grinning? I don't find this amusing at all."

Robbie stuck his head out and said, "We tried to warn you, Alex, but you didn't believe us."

"Of course I did not. I never thought my wife to blatantly disobey my order. She'll pay for it, you can be certain."

"Your order?" Logan guffawed. "Say that word to Gwynie, and she'll knock you down with a fist."

Alex scowled, trying to understand Logan's words. "A wife's job is to obey her husband. The church commands it."

"Mayhap you're correct, but I don't order Celestina around," Brodie said.

"Why are you afraid to give your wives orders?"

"'Tis not fear, Alex," Robbie said, "but respect. Caralyn says giving her orders all the time reminds her of her former life."

"Celestina says the same. Her father never allowed her to question his commands. Ever. She cries if I bark an order at her. She said it takes her back to being held prisoner by her own father."

Alex hadn't considered that before. Would Maddie feel the same about any order? His orders weren't cruel or inhumane as Kenneth's had been, so he'd felt they were acceptable to make. It was the way of marriage. But Maddie had compared him to that terrible man yesterday. At the time, he'd thought she'd spoken only in anger, but perhaps his ordering was too much of a reminder for her.

"And you'll not be going after Mac," Brodie said. "I heard your threat earlier. I'll stand by his side, and you know why."

Alex did know why. In truth, he thanked the Lord above for Mac. It'd been Mac that had sent him that message years ago that the bastard Kenneth beat his sister. Without it, he might never have returned to MacDonald keep, and Maddie would not have grabbed a piece of his soul with one glance.

Brodie had been with Alex when he'd received the letter that spurred their return to the castle, and he knew well Mac's role in it. He'd always respected the man for that.

"I know, Brodie. I recall it well. Mac's only protecting her. I spoke through rage."

"Aye, but we need to move, Grant," Logan said, grumbling while he paced. "There's a storm on its way."

Alex nodded, shifting to strategic thought. He

had to be prepared for any circumstance. "Robbie, you're willing to stay back? If they've gotten to a certain point, we'll go on to Ramsay land and not return until after the Yule."

"Aye, you know we'll stay here."

"I'm leaving now with twenty warriors. Send another two score behind us, but have them bring two carts, just in case 'tis needed."

"I think 'tis wise," Robbie said.

"Why are the carts needed?" Logan asked.

"Maddie is strong," Alex said. "So strong that she'll not let on if she needs help. She'll drive herself until she falls off the horse, before which you'd never have known anything was wrong. And then we must also think of Alice and the bairns. None of them had to travel in cold like this before."

"I understand."

Alex grew anxious to leave. He turned to Brodie. "I don't worry about the lads, but I do worry about the wee lassie. I'll feel better when I can get her against my chest. Get Loki and come with us now. Or travel with Celestina and the remaining warriors and follow us."

Loki was Brodie and Celestina's adopted son. Brodie had found him living in a crate behind a tavern in the royal burgh. A cheeky lad who'd always known all that went on in the burgh, he'd proven invaluable to Brodie and Nicol when they'd been searching for Celestina when her stepfather and first husband had placed her in hiding. After all he'd done to assist them, they'd brought him back to Grant land and adopted him.

"I'm sure she'll wish to come but I'd prefer she follow with the second group, and Inga will probably join her. Nicol and I will come with you," Brodie replied. "And we'll want Loki with us. He can be a clever lad."

"Aye, I will. Where's the lad?"

"I have not seen him this morning. Have any of you?"

An idea sparked in Alex's mind, and without another word, he made his way to the stables, Brodie, Logan, and Robbie on his heels. Alex stepped inside, surveying the horses in the stalls, and was pleased with what he found.

"What is it?" Brodie asked, coming in behind him.

"Mac made sure they took the strongest horses, but there's another missing."

His brother glanced over the stalls. "Loki's horse."

"Aye, my guess is Loki followed them. And if the lad stays true to his nature, he'll be returning with some information that could help us. If we find Loki, then we may find which path the others took out of the mountains."

Brodie grinned, his chest puffing out a bit over the compliment Alex had given his son. But Alex didn't think any of them were surprised. Loki had proven to be cleverer than most over and over again.

Alex led his horse Midnight out of the stall, loaded up the supplies Brodie still carried, and grabbed two apples. Then he lifted one of Maddie's scarves off the peg on the wall and held it up to Midnight's nose. "We have to find her."

Midnight whinnied and took the apple in one bite just before Alex mounted and flicked the reins.

They were on the hunt.

⸻

When Mac had helped Alice to dismount at the mouth of the cave, her knees buckled, nearly taking her to the ground. Maddie quickly set Jamie down and grabbed Kyla from her maid's iron grip. "I have her, Alice. Let go."

Alice released Kyla and grabbed onto her husband as he helped her to stay upright.

"What's wrong, Alice?" Maddie's question came out in a near shout of panic. "Are you sick?"

Mac shook his head at Maddie. "'Tis what happens with old limbs, lass. It you don't move them for a time, they'll tighten up on you. She'll be fine in a moment."

Maddie felt the tension in her shoulders ease. She trusted Mac's word.

"Jake, Jamie, follow me into the cave." She grabbed her horse's reins and led him toward the cave, hoping to keep their belongings dry.

"Go around the bend, Maddie. The horses can stay in the front. I'll put Alice on the rock ledge at the bend, then start the fire."

The lads ran ahead of her, though it was no surprise to her. They were adventurous laddies and loved exploring anything in the wilderness.

"Lads, not too far back. Find the ledge for Mac

so he knows where to set Alice." Giving them a chore was always the best tactic.

Kyla giggled and tipped her head back, sticking her tongue out to catch the snowflakes, now swirling around them. "Sno'."

Most of her words were abbreviated versions of the correct word, but she managed to get her point across.

"Aye, lots of snowflakes for you. We're going inside to look for the lads."

Kyla wriggled in her arms once they stepped into the cave. "Down."

"Of course, you wish to get down." She set her daughter down and sighed, watching her chase after her brothers. Maddie spun around to see where Mac was, glad to see him not far behind her. Alice was moving slowly beside him, but moving, and the other two horses followed Maddie's horse toward the cave. She grabbed the bag of food from one saddle and followed the boys inside the cave and around the bend.

The cave was perfect for their wait. The sun was up, so she had to guess the men would find them within a few hours, based on the fact that the guards could travel faster than they had. "How did you know this was here, Mac?"

"'Tis the cave all the Grants and Ramsays use. If they pass by, your husband will check for us here. I'm sure of it. We're not moving until Logan or your husband find us, lass."

She used her dagger to cut an apple into pieces and gave each of the bairns a wedge to chew on while she moved back to the horses. They would need more furs and plaids, especially for poor Alice.

Staring out over the landscape, she watched the whirling snow, the storm becoming a beastly thing as the wind picked up, the visibility decreasing.

Perhaps she'd been too hasty in her decision to travel on their own.

"Lads, you'll come out to relieve yourselves now." She'd go with them, before the snow became too deep and the visibility worsened. "Kyla, you'll stay with Alice."

"Maddie, look for any dry wood before it gets buried beneath the snow," Mac called out. "There's a spot around the side where it often sits."

The boys chuckled and chased ahead of her, more than happy to aim their pee into a snowbank to turn it yellow. As always, they competed.

"Mine went farther, Jake."

"Nay, I drew a sun in the snow. 'Tis why mine didn't go as far."

Maddie shook her head and pointed back to the cave once they finished. The two rambunctious boys raced each other back. She pulled her scarf over her face and looked for any wood at all, surprised to see a small pile hidden under a clump of bushes. Hoping it would be enough, she grabbed the wood and carried it inside, clutching it against her chest.

"I found this, Mac," she said, dropping the wood in the spot where Mac pointed.

"Good. Usually the Grants also leave a small

pile of wood in here, in case of rain." He followed the cave back into the dark recesses where she couldn't see him, but he returned quickly with wood in his arms. "Between the two, we've enough."

"You believe Alex will know to stop here?"

"Aye, surely he will." Mac bent down to start the fire closer to the mouth of the cave, struggling at first, but he managed to get it going.

That's when Maddie noticed Alice was still shivering. She ransacked the bags for more furs and found two, removing them and covering Alice's lap. "Alice, you're trembling."

"I'm not used to this cold, Maddie, but I'll be fine once the fire is going. Do not worry on me. Take care of the bairns. Get them fed. I'll be able to change Kyla's rag in a moment."

Alice would not like her fussing over her more than she already had, and it was true that the cave, while warmer, was still cold. The fire would surely settle her shivering. So Maddie covered her up and set herself after the lads and Kyla while Mac took care of the horses.

She couldn't help but notice how the bairns adjusted to the situation and the cold with such speed, but she, Mac, and Alice were not so quick. Her own hands were freezing, and she moved to the fire to warm them before she changed Kyla's rag. Of course, the wee lass didn't wish to be changed at all.

"Lads, come distract your sister while I tend to her rag."

They did as she asked and brought over two

pinecones for Kyla to play with, which kept her on her back and still, in contrast to her usual escape attempts. At one point, Kayla stopped to scowl at her mother and said, "Mama. Col'."

"I know you are cold, my sweeting. We'll be done soon. You'll feel better in a dry garment."

Once she finished, she couldn't stop herself from going back to the mouth of the cave to stare out. *Patience* was not a word used to describe her. Oh, she was patient with bairns and the elderly, but when she wished for something, she did not relish waiting around for it. It usually was not long before she went after it herself. Alex had better hurry.

She smiled to herself then.

She'd started the journey running away from her husband with all the speed she could muster. Now she found herself feeling rushed to be found.

What exactly was Alex thinking at this moment?

CHAPTER SEVEN

"GOD'S BONES, IT'S not like she has many choices, Grant. She would take the ravine because 'tis faster," Logan shouted.

Alex had been arguing with him over which way Mac would have taken Maddie.

"It's faster, aye, but not nearly as safe. Would Mac have risked it?"

"With Maddie hastening him, I'd say he would have. They would have been here earlier, before this heavy snowfall."

"The wind is strengthening, and we'll be in a full storm before long," Alex said.

Brodie nodded. "We need to cross the ravine before that. We'll not be able to see where we're going soon, and it's a long fall down if we attempt it then."

Alex nodded, silently cursing his wife's stubborn nature. Or was it his own stubborn nature that was at fault this time? He'd not explained his reasoning well, instead expecting Maddie to do whatever he said without question. Brenna had warned him once that his ideas were outmoded and daft at times.

His thoughts were interrupted when he noticed a horse coming toward them.

He knew Logan saw the same, because he pointed toward it in the distance and said, "Here comes the missing lad. Mayhap he has news for us."

Loki's horse galloped straight toward them, the lad's excitement visible even from a distance.

Brodie yelled out to him, "I'll chastise you later for going off on your own, but what have you for us? You've discovered something, have you not?"

"Aye," he said, pausing to catch his breath. "They went through the ravine. I checked which way they were going, then came back to tell you. I'll bet they're in the cave by now."

"Aye, if Mac is wise enough not to listen to my stubborn wife, who I'm sure wanted to press on." Alex cursed under his breath again, then remembered to thank Loki. "I'm pleased you were so resourceful, lad."

Logan said, "She'll stop in the cave, Grant. Her goal was to get far enough that you'd have to take her to Ramsay land. And as you said before, she's not used to traveling for that long. She'll be freezing."

"I'm not sure that cave would be considered halfway," Alex said, his lips pursed tight to keep himself from launching into another tirade. How the hell could Maddie have done something so foolish? No matter how he tried, he couldn't come up with any sound reason for her to act so rashly with their bairns and Alice and Mac. Being foolish over her own comforts was one thing, but to risk the young and the elderly was beyond something he thought her capable of doing. Even if he had ordered her around, she knew better.

Logan snorted. "After several hours in this weather with three bairns, she'll be wishing it's more than halfway."

Alex cast a sideways glance at Logan, knowing he was right.

Still, his concern over how they were faring in this storm only grew. He worried especially for Kyla and Alice.

"Let's move on. Loki, lead the way."

They headed off toward the ravine, the wind swirling flakes in their face. He was glad he'd allowed his beard to grow for the winter. It was rough against Maddie's tender skin, but Kyla loved it, giggling and squealing with delight every time she touched it.

He'd told his wife as much only a sennight ago, while holding a giggling Kyla.

Maddie had rolled her eyes and smiled. "I know it keeps your face warm in this weather. I'll survive."

Then she'd kissed his cheek while Kyla giggled even more.

"Kiss," the wee lass had said, touching his lips.

He'd kissed her as carefully as possible, not wanting his beard to scratch her delicate skin, and she'd still broken into a fit of giggles.

After she'd calmed, she had pointed at the door and said, "'Side," with the quiet confidence of a child who knows her request will be met.

His daughter loved the outdoors even at such a young age.

He'd cast a glance to Maddie, who had nodded, so then he'd done his favorite task of all: wrapped the lass against his chest and headed out to the stables, her favorite place. He loved having her wrapped so closely against him so he was able to inhale her sweet scent as he carried her to see the horses.

Another gust of wind and snow brought him out of memory and back to the ravine.

They'd find them. They would find them all, and all would be well, and his sweet lassie would be against his chest again.

He couldn't consider the alternative.

Maddie awakened to a sound she didn't recognize. Even though it had been daylight, they'd fallen asleep, probably because they'd been up the night before. Most of the night for the adults, half the night for the bairns. Now she had no idea what time of day it was because the storm kept the sun nearly invisible.

Bolting up in the cave, grateful for the fur beneath her to keep her backside warm, she focused, trembling from the quick onset of cold once the plaid dropped off her shoulders.

She checked on the three bairns beside her first. Kyla slept soundly between the twins, the lads' heat more than enough for her. She lowered her face to each forehead, planting a kiss on each of her three babes to check for fever, satisfying her need to make sure they were safe and warm.

She looked around. The embers from the fire still threw off some heat, and the horses in the mouth of the cave blocked much of the wind.

No wonder Clan Grant and Ramsay both preferred this cave. It was perfect.

But what was the odd sound that had awakened her?

Glancing back over her shoulder, she paused to listen until she deciphered the source of the strange noise—Alice's teeth chattering against themselves. Curled up next to her husband, she still trembled in the cold.

Maddie got up and found a fur that had fallen from around the two of them, carefully placing it over the mound of their bodies so as not to awaken either one. She rearranged the fur covering Alice's feet, noticing it had also fallen away, leaving their woolen socks and boots open to the cold. Once she had everything rearranged, she knew what she had to do next.

First she had to satisfy her natural urge, so she moved to the mouth of the cave, reached down to the pile of leaves they'd gathered before the snow had covered the ground, and took two before heading outside. She stopped next to her dear horse, nuzzling her sweetly with a pat before turning her attention to the weather conditions she was about to enter.

The wind had slowed a bit, giving her the incentive to relieve herself when she wouldn't freeze to death. The hoot of a distant owl echoed across the white landscape, the sun reflecting off the snow as if they lived in the land of the ice.

She'd heard of lands where people lived in snow much of the time, building houses of ice and other natural elements. Could she ever survive in such a land? She thought not.

She made her way to a protected spot in the woods, made quick with her task, and rinsed her hands in the cold snow before stuffing a few handfuls into her mouth to refresh herself. Her hood fell back, and she tugged on the shawl she had underneath, tightening it around her face as she trudged toward the cave. It was terribly cold. The thought of leaning against the heat of her husband made her sigh with yearning, but she pushed it aside for now.

Alice's chattering teeth came to mind again. Was her maid in danger? They could not seem to get her warm.

She knew Alex and Logan would be somewhere nearby looking for them. Why hadn't they arrived? They should have by now. Had the storm prevented them from finding the trail?

Perhaps it was time for her to go out on her own to find them.

She approached the mouth of the cave, still in deep thought, when a sound called out to her—a delicious sound she'd been praying for all night. A horse crossed the periphery of her vision. But when she turned toward it, the person seated was not who she expected to see. It was not Alex or Logan, but someone much smaller.

"Loki?" she called out, wishing to yell as loud as she could but not wanting to awaken the others.

"Loki?" she repeated, following the form that had disappeared down the main path. She ran, huffing at having to lift her feet in the snow, a task that took significantly more effort than one would expect.

"Loki!" Her bellow at the main path should have been heard, but his horse was moving too quickly.

She spun around, looking for any others, but saw none. She had only moments to make up her mind. Alice's health was in danger, she knew. She should not be as chilled as she was; something was wrong. And that blame was hers—she shouldn't have coerced Mac and Alice to come along with her.

This could be her only chance to catch someone to help them.

Moving back to the mouth of the cave, she led her horse out and mounted it, flicking the reins and sending the beast to the main path so she could catch up with Loki. The lad would surely know where to find Logan and Alex.

She caught a glimpse of the tracks and followed them, pushing her horse hard to catch him. She called out as she flew down the path, but the falling snow swallowed her voice. She was dismayed that his figure only traveled farther away, her animal unable to gain ground on his. The snow fell heavier now, and she was losing sight of Loki. The swirl of flakes hid the tracks of his horse's hooves until she could no longer follow.

Maddie shivered, slowing her horse. She'd have to go back to the cave and wait for another chance, for someone else to ride by the entrance. But when she turned the animal around, she discovered something that threaded ice through her veins.

She could no longer see the path she'd followed, and she had no idea how far she'd traveled in her haste to catch Loki. In the blinding snow, she didn't know which way to go.

How would she ever find her way back?

CHAPTER EIGHT

THEY MET AT the other side of the ravine, the swirling snow preventing them from seeing much ahead of them.

"Hell, but could you not stop long enough for us to find them?" Alex bellowed, his head tipped back to yell at the snow.

Logan only arched his brow, now caked with ice. "Curse the snow if you wish, Grant, but we must move along. Curse while moving."

Alex grumbled, still cursing himself, his wife, and anything else related to his current predicament.

Brodie suddenly spoke. "We need to split up."

"Nay," Alex said. "We all go to the cave together first, see if there is any evidence they've been there."

"They should be there because if they left in the middle of the night, they'll need sleep. We'll reach the cave shortly after the sun is high. Likely they'll all be awakening then," Logan said. "Where did Loki go?"

Brodie shrugged his shoulders. "He wished to

travel ahead a bit, search out the area past the cave while we search the cave. He set off after landing on this side of the ravine."

"He's an odd wandering lad," Logan said. "Will he be able to find his way?"

Alex said, "He has good instincts and good tracking. He'll find our group again. Now, we need to move before the snow piles higher and makes it too difficult for the horses to travel."

Mac stirred and peered out toward the mouth of the cave. High sun was upon them, but something wasn't right. Then he discovered what it was. A wee lassie's face appeared in front of him, smiling. "Mama?" Kyla asked.

A lad was directly behind the lass. "Mama's gone, Mac. Where would she be?"

Jamie's face held a look Mac didn't often see from the lad—worry was etched on his features.

Mac pushed himself to a sitting position, then took the fur and wrapped it around Alice, who was still sleeping soundly. "She's probably taking care of her needs, lad. Give her a moment or two. I'm sure she'll return."

"I don't think so," Jake said, running to the entrance of the cave and back. "She took her horse."

A sense of gloom and foreboding overcame Mac then. Surely she wouldn't have. She couldn't have been so foolish as to go search out her husband or Logan herself, could she?

"Are you certain her horse is gone, lad?"

Jamie ran to the horses this time. "Aye, it's gone."

Kyla echoed, "Gone."

"I'll go look," Mac said gruffly. "You all stay here."

"But I have to pish," Jake declared, looking up at Mac with a look that reminded him of the lad's father.

"Me too."

Alice woke up then. "What's wrong, Mac?"

"Maddie isn't here, but I'm hoping she's just gone nearby in search of firewood. The lads and I will go check. You keep Kyla with you."

Alice picked up the little lass and said, "Och! Someone needs a clean rag. I'll take care of it while you go."

"Come with me, lads."

He quickly took care of his own needs, then walked in a wide arc, making a point to move out toward the path to check for any sign of Maddie.

There was none.

The two lads had scampered out into the wilderness behind Mac, likely searching the area for their mother. Mac couldn't help but wonder what would go through the minds of lads at their tender age when their mother took them on a journey without their father. Instead, he watched the two compete over who could leave the longest trail of yellow in the snow.

Oh, but to be young again.

Mac walked the wider path again, hoping to see any sign of Maddie. He did not. Maddie had left on her own, going far enough to be in need of a horse. He scratched his beard and wondered what he was to do next. If she couldn't find her husband, she would be out there alone, and she was surely not resourceful enough to locate another cave in this storm. Would she even be able to find her way back?

Alex would kill him for letting her out of his sight.

And his guilt would kill him if he did not go after her now. Not to mention that he had a soft spot for the lass ever since he'd married Alice. She had the biggest heart of anyone he knew, so he had to find her.

He made his way back inside the cave.

His wife's hopeful expression nearly undid him, simply because he hated disappointing her. She was devoted to her mistress, and this would upset her terribly.

"Did you find her?"

"Nay. She's nowhere to be found." He sat on a stone ledge close to her. "Alice, I think I must go after her, at least a short distance. The snow has let up a wee bit, so I think 'tis important that I check the immediate area, though I hate to leave you alone."

"I'll go along," Jake shouted.

"Nay, I'm going with him. You stay here, Jake."

"Mac, you'll have to take them both along. If you leave them behind, they'll sneak away on me, and we'll be missing another. But don't go too far. Just a bit to see if you can find her."

Mac signed, leaning over to kiss his wife's forehead. "I fear you are right. They could be a help to me as their eyes are better than my old ones."

"Kyla and I will be fine."

"I'll leave you two extra furs, stir the fire up for you with more wood. And I'll fill the skein with fresh water. You have food yet, aye?"

"Aye, we have plenty. Take the oatcakes and the dried meat. We'll eat the cheese and the bread."

The two stared at each other.

Mac finally said, "I think we made a mistake, Alice. But I promise to return quickly."

Tears misted his wife's eyes, so he told a wee fib. "I'm certain I'll find her. Do not fret. Mayhap I will find Alex Grant while we're out, as well."

As Alice nodded, smiling weakly, Mac said a quick prayer for a miracle.

CHAPTER NINE

THE SUN WAS high and peeking through the clouds occasionally, a sign the storm could be abating. If the snow would stop, she'd have a better chance to find her way back to the cave. Hunger gnawed at the inside of her belly, reminding her that she had not eaten upon waking.

Was it Loki on that horse?

Doubt snaked its way through her. What if it was some other rider? Or an apparition or wishful vision of her mind?

She did not know any longer who or what she'd been chasing, only that it'd been for naught.

The wind came up again, whistling through the pines and swirling the snow around her face, making her trek even more difficult. She continued to head in the same direction only because she didn't wish to travel in circles.

She'd decided that she must either be traveling toward Loki or headed back to Grant land, or both. She dismissed the fear that she could have taken a turn off the main path and now be lost where no one would ever think to look.

Excitement coursed through her as she saw an outcropping ahead, one that looked like the ravine they'd traveled through before entering the cave. If it proved to be the same ravine, she would be headed in the direction of Clan Grant.

She could be headed straight for a Grant patrol. Straight for Alex!

At the moment, the thought of reuniting with him was pure bliss.

Why had she been so foolish as to do this on her own? She'd risked the lives of her bairns. And two dear friends. And herself.

She fought the tears because she didn't want them freezing on her cheekbones. She'd been a fool. "I'm sorry, Mama. I was foolish. Please send someone to help me." She'd had a dream of her mother at another time when she'd felt desperate. Perhaps she could help her again. If her father were here, he'd be chastising her for acting without thinking, for letting a demented man's past actions twist her thinking in the wrong way.

Under no circumstances did Alexander Grant have any characteristics similar to Kenneth. They were not alike.

At all.

She'd allowed her desire to see their bairns have a wonderful holiday with the Ramsays overshadow her clear thinking. That and the need to have some say in the decisions she made with her husband. It was supposed to be a marriage in which they shared decisions.

Fear and memories of horrible times made her quite protective of her freedom. But she'd not been fair enough to all involved in this decision, instead making them part of this small battle with her husband.

She had to pray Alex would come soon. He would, wouldn't he?

But she knew Alex would find them. Or Logan would find them. Or Loki would find them. Someone would surely find them, and all would be well.

She hurried her horse toward the edge of the ravine, the hope building inside her so much that she wished to squeal with happiness.

She'd apologize to Alex, to Logan, and especially to Mac and Alice.

Should she wait at the end of the ravine for the patrol? But what if the men had already come and gone? No, if she did not spot them crossing, she'd slowly turn around and locate the cave again. She remembered the way from the ravine. And Mac may be outside the cave entrance looking for her, which would make spotting it simpler. Then, at least, she'd be back with her bairns and her two beloved friends to wait for Alex.

Reaching the edge of the ravine, she slowed her horse to assess the situation—then broke out in tears.

It was not the ravine they'd passed through, so she couldn't cross it. Who knew how long it was or what she'd find on the other end? It was completely new to her. So new that she realized how well and truly lost she was.

Tears flooded her face, freezing in spots. The wind picked up, so she wrapped her scarf around her face as tight as she could, doing her best to stop her tears, but she couldn't. She was lost, so utterly lost, and in the middle of a storm that covered all tracks and paths. Turning her mount around, she headed away from the dangerous ravine and, tipping her head back, let out a wail of mourning. She feared she'd die here in this unknown place, cold and lost. She stopped her mare where they stood and sobbed, allowing herself to cry for her foolishness, for her bairns and friends, for her dearest husband whom she loved with all her heart.

Someone took the reins from her hands, and her eyes flew open, peering at the group in front of her. Four horses led her down a path. She could not see the first rider, but the second had long dark hair waving in the wind.

"Alex?"

There was no response. Had the wind taken her question?

She glanced at the other two riders closest to her. The one who held the reins had blond hair like Robbie, and the other had red hair the likes of which she'd only seen on Alex's guard, Nicol.

"Robbie? Nicol? Alex?" she asked again, louder this time, sure they heard her.

Silence met her once again and fear tightened her belly.

"Who are you? Tell me where you're taking me!" she bellowed, doing her best to sound more angry than afraid. "I demand you release me!"

But the four ignored her and she was powerless. She did not have the strength to regain her reins from the blond-haired rider, to fight them all. The wind came up again, so she dropped her head, protecting her face from the cold. Her best hope was that they could be from a neighboring clan—the Camerons, the Menzies—rather than malicious in their intent. Mayhap they'd take her inside their keep, set her in front of a nice hearth, cover her with a fur, and offer her a steaming cup of broth to drink. Yet, if they were friendly, then why the silence?

She did not know.

She only prayed they would lead her somewhere safe and warm before she lost her remaining senses.

She was so very cold. Her eyes grew heavy then, and she struggled to remain upright on her horse.

Whoever these four men were, she had to trust them.

She didn't have the strength for anything else.

Mac set the lads on the horse, then mounted behind them. "Remember your promise, lads?"

"Aye, Mac," Jamie said. "We'll do whatever you tell us. We promise to be good."

"Aye," Jake said, staring up at him with excitement. "And I'll look for any sign of Mama or her horse. We'll find her because we are Grant warriors." The lad pounded his chest for emphasis on the last word.

Mac thought it was a good thing they were young enough not to know what was really happening, that it seemed exciting rather than the nightmare it was.

"And the third promise?"

The boys answered in unison. "Do not go off alone."

Mac flicked the reins of his horse and set off in the direction he guessed Maddie would have gone. "Look for any sign of a horse traveling. Hoofprints, horse droppings."

"We're on an adventure," Jamie said.

"And Papa will be proud of us."

"'Cause we'll find Mama."

"And bring her back to Papa."

"I'll see her first." Jake smirked at his brother, glancing back over his shoulder.

"Nay, I'll find her first, Jake."

"Jamie, I can see better than you."

"But I'm smarter than you."

"I'm better at swordplay."

"I'm a faster runner."

"But I—"

"Lads!"

The two stopped and looked back over their shoulders at Mac.

The lads would make him tear each of the remaining hairs out of his head one by one if they continued with this. "Rule number four: No arguing."

"Awww," Jamie said.

Jake said, "'Tis your fault, Jamie."

"'Tis not!"

Mac cleared his throat. Both lads finally quieted.

Mac let out a deep breath. Perhaps he'd be able

to think now.

Not a moment later, Jake's hand shot out at the same time as Jamie's, but Mac had no idea what they were pointing at. "What is it?"

"Midnight," Jamie said.

Jake broke out in a huge grin. "Aye, 'tis Papa's horse!"

CHAPTER TEN

WHEN MADDIE AWAKENED, the dark-haired man gently helped her down from the horse. She brushed the stray hairs out of her eyes and looked up at him.

She blinked. "Alex?"

"Nay, not Alex."

At first glance, the man bore a remarkable resemblance to her husband, right down to the same gray eyes. On closer inspection, she realized that he wasn't as tall as Alex, and he had a mole on his neck that her husband didn't have, but he definitely could have been a brother. Did Alex have one she didn't know about?

"Who are you?" she asked. "And why do you look so much like my husband?"

"My name is Alasdair." He set her feet down in the snow and her knees buckled, but he caught her. "And you are not the first to compare me to Alex Grant."

"Alasdair, you need to get her inside," the second man interrupted, his red locks swirling about his face. He had the greenest eyes she'd ever seen.

The blond man then came up to her right side and took her elbow. "Here, I'll help you inside. Then we'll start a fire and cover you up. You must warm up immediately. You were out too long in this storm."

"Who are you?" Maddie asked, staring up into his crystal blue eyes.

"You may call me Els, short for Elshander. Now, inside."

Maddie felt no need to resist these men. Something about them was familiar somehow, and she felt no fear around them. Though, given how weak she felt, she wasn't sure she could fight them even if she didn't feel such peace. Her mother had always told her that she should follow her instincts in life, that they would never fail her.

Right now, her instinct was to do whatever these four men suggested. Being alone on unfamiliar land was far from safe, and this group offered her the only alternative at present, so it was probably best to go along with them.

The men helped her inside a cave. It was not as large as the one she'd left behind, but it still would protect her from the wind. The fourth man took her horse and led the beast around the side of the outcropping, presumably where it would be protected.

Els led her to a rock where she could sit down. When she did, she felt as if she became even heavier somehow, as if her limbs were slowly filling with stone. Her shivering hadn't abated yet, and even though she was protected against the wind, her fingers and toes were turning numb, and her thinking slowed. Had she fallen asleep and dreamed this group?

She didn't know what to believe anymore. A day ago she'd been in her great hall with her family and friends, enjoying her bairns. Now she was lost in a storm and alone.

Then the red-haired man brought in a stack of dry wood, piled it on the stone floor, and blew on it. The kindling blossomed into flames.

She gasped. "How did you do that?"

He smiled at her. "I only lit the fire."

"But how . . ." Maddie trailed off, wondering if her tired eyes were playing tricks on her. She felt heavy and cold, even with the fire beside her. Mayhap her exhaustion was causing visions.

"And what is your name?" she asked instead.

"Alick."

"Where did you hail from, Alick? What clan?"

"That doesn't matter," Alasdair interrupted. "What does matter is that we get your body warm. We have some cheese for you, for sustenance. You must build your strength back. You've lost much."

She took the hunk of cheese and took a bite, moaning at the sweet taste of it. "This is delicious," she mumbled between chews. When she finished, she asked, "Where am I?"

Els said, "In a cave nearing Ramsay land. Alex will find you, but it will be a bit yet. In the meantime, we'll wrap you in furs, get you something to drink, and keep the fire going. We will do what we can, but Alex must do the rest. He is your protector."

"The rest? What must Alex do?"

"Worry not. Just rest and think of how soon you'll be with your bairns again."

Alick came forward with a pile of furs and arranged them in such a manner that she could lie down, something that was oddly enticing even though she'd woken from a nap just a few hours before. As if reading her thoughts, Alick said, "Aye, the cold has drained you and all your will. The storm has a force to it that you cannot see. But it has also drained your belief in your husband. The two of you are so powerful together. You will build a formidable clan, but you must join together to do this. We're here to see that it does happen, that nothing will get in the way. You need rest. Sleep until Alex finds you and warms you."

She didn't understand all he said—how could a mere storm have power over her will?—but something in her simply trusted his advice. And what did he mean by what they would do, about building a powerful clan? How could he know what would happen years from now?

At the moment, she could not think on this puzzle any longer because she was tired. Too tired, too cold, too worried, too everything . . .

So she rested herself on the warm furs with a sigh, lying on her side and tucking her legs up tight to her chest. Alick covered her with furs, and she closed her eyes, more tired than she could bear.

She heard the fourth man reenter the cave. "Your horse is on the side of the cave. I gave him some oats."

Maddie's eyes reopened. That was the voice of a woman, not a man.

And sure enough, a woman knelt next to her.

"You're not a man. You're a woman. A beautiful one," Maddie said.

The woman smiled and patted her shoulder, her white-blonde hair falling forward. "We must go now. But do not worry. He'll find you if you wait for him here."

"Go? Why? Please don't leave me." She felt safe with these strangers who emanated an odd sense of calm. Then something dawned on her. "You seem so certain Alex will find me. Why?"

"Let us say that we know a bit of the future," Alasdair said, looking around at the others, who chuckled. "But we must go now. We're only allowed a short time with you, and we must hurry him along."

Maddie's eyes felt heavy, but she forced them to remain open. She still had no idea who these people were, or their reasons for aiding her. "The future? Who are you, and why are you helping me? Please tell me."

It was the woman who smiled. "Ach, I will tell her. Someday you will meet us, and we will spend much time together. We've had to come to your assistance because there was no alternative. 'Tis our job to watch over you both for the next several years. Until we can meet." She leaned close to Maddie then and whispered, "These are your grandsons, and I'm your granddaughter. My sire will be your last son, whom you'll name Connor.

And we four have come back to this day and time to help you. Consider us your guardian angels."

Maddie swallowed, the woman's words bouncing around her befuddled mind and only adding to her confusion. Was she daft? What she said was not possible. And yet, sincerity shone brightly from her face.

Maddie reached up to touch the lass's face, taking in everything about her. "You look like Alex with white hair, and you have my eyes. I suppose 'tis possible. I have to believe you because I have no other explanation. Am I going to die? Is that why you've come?"

"We've come to make sure that doesn't happen, to make sure you survive until Alex finds you. He must save you. You will have many children and many grandchildren. Your heart is plenty big enough to love us all. But do not dismiss that Alex needs you too." Maddie glanced at Alasdair, who so looked like Alex, then at Alick, who'd lit a fire with his breath alone. She knew not what magick this may be, but in that moment, she decided to trust it. She had so many questions, and yet all she could mutter was, "Why? Why help me now?"

"Because if we didn't help to save you today, Grandmama, I'd never exist. You must survive this storm because you have more bairns and many more grandchildren to come. I know your will has been drained from you, but you must not let go. You must wait for Grandda and fight until then."

"You will leave the fire for me?"

"We will, but it will go out. We must get

Grandda here quickly. 'Tis our next task."

Maddie absorbed the words, knowing the lass spoke the truth. For although she'd been warmed on the outside by the fire, inside she felt the cold had yet to thaw. And it was a cold that drained her greatly, pulling her to sleep. Her eyes began to shut, but she pushed out one final question.

"What is your name?"

"My name is Dyna. And my father is right here." She patted Maddie's belly.

Alex held his breath while they moved toward the cave the Grant warriors knew so well. He'd taken Mac there on a couple of occasions, so he prayed the old man had stopped here to wait out the storm. The snowfall had stopped for a while, allowing them to make good time to the cave, but now it was picking up again. Big fat snowflakes impeded their view, especially when the wind blew harder, tricking them into making wrong turns.

He was thankful they were now so close. But on the heels of his gratitude was his uncertainty.

He had a decision to make before they arrived. How would he react once he knew Maddie and the bairns were safe? He knew his instinct would be to grab all four of them and hold them close, yet he was not so sure that his anger at Maddie wouldn't flare. He was furious that she had ignored his command, and he thought the desire to embrace her and throttle her at the same time would cause him to say something he would regret.

And Maddie? How would she react? Would she be glad to see him now or upset that he'd refused her request and forced her hand?

He could embrace the bairns without conflict at least. He prayed again that they would all be safely ensconced inside the cave.

Brodie and Loki were ahead of him, Logan next to him. A whinny echoed through the wind to them. There, in the mouth of the cave, stood one of the Grant mares. They were here.

The relief was like a punch in the gut.

As soon as he got over that punch, another worrisome one followed. They surely didn't all get here on one horse. Where the hell were the others?

He scanned the area, but nothing told him where the others were.

Brodie turned to look at him and said, "Someone is here. We'll find out where the others are soon enough. No reason to panic yet, Alex."

Loki was already off his horse and running into the cave.

Alex dismounted, handing one of the guards the reins of his horse and indicating they were to stay back. He stepped inside the cave and froze, his heart plummeting to his toes. There were only two people inside: Alice and Kyla.

Alice shivered in the corner, near what had once been a fire but was now just embers. Kyla played with a stick, trying to move a stone about the area. She glanced up at her father as soon as he stepped inside.

Whatever had happened, he would first start a fire. Alice needed heat, and even Kyla looked like she was nearly shivering, though she was well wrapped in furs.

Kyla waddled over to Alex and held her hands up to him, her slightly blue lips smiling but trembling just the same. "Up, Da."

When Alex lifted her, he realized her rag felt heavy. Alice spoke up right away. "I changed her right before Mac left, but I think she may need changing again. My hands cannot do it, Alex. Please change her raggie."

"Many thanks for all you've done, Alice. I'll take care of her." He wanted to ask, "Where were Maddie and the lads? And Mac?" But he could see Alice needed warming right away. His questions could wait.

Logan joined him and immediately jumped in to help Alex change Kyla's rag, grabbing a dry one from a sack in the corner. "You don't know how to do this right, Grant. I'll do it." He had the bairn out of her clothes quickly while Alex held her against his chest. Kyla giggled when the cold air hit her, then frowned as if wondering what was happening to her. Logan stripped her down to her wet rag and ripped it off her, taking her from Alex to run her quickly to the snow to wash her bottom.

"Uncle Logan is fixing your rag, Kyla. I'll warm you in a moment." She never cried, but then again, Alex had never seen anyone change a rag as quickly as Logan did now. "You have special talents, Logan."

"'Tis only one of many you don't know about. She is cold. She's going against your chest, Grant, and I mean inside your mantle and tunic."

Alex nodded, as he was thinking the same.

Poor Kyla began to cry and shiver while Logan cleaned her, but that gave Alex time to loosen his clothing and tie his plaid just so to hold her in place against his chest. As Logan wrapped a small fur under Kyla so that she wouldn't pish all over them both, Alex knelt down beside Alice, who was racked with shivers, her teeth chattering, her eyes now closed. "Alice?"

Alice's eyes briefly opened, widening when they focused on him and then on the empty fur beside her. "Kyla? You've changed her?"

"Aye, we have her, Alice."

Logan approached with Kyla, and Alex stood and grabbed her, placing a kiss on her forehead and tucking her against his skin. He did his best to control his own shudders at her temperature, as she settled against him with a sigh and a smile.

"I'll warm you, sweeting."

"Milk?"

"I gave her cheese, but she wants her milk, Alex," Alice said through her trembling jaw.

Milk. Of course, the lass was hungry. "Brodie, did you bring anything for the bairns to eat or drink?"

"Aye, I filled a skein with goat's milk." Brodie returned to his horse and brought two skeins inside, handing one to Alex. "The other is ale. I think Loki has one of water."

"Make sure Alice takes some of that ale while I

give this to my wee one."

Alex helped Kyla sip the milk. She drank heavily, then pushed the half-empty skein away before snuggling against him and falling fast asleep.

Alex then knelt down in front of a still shivering Alice, while Logan gave instructions for men to get firewood so they could start a fire. "Where did they go, Alice?"

Alice began to cry. "Maddie left alone before dawn. Mac and the lads went after her."

Shite.

They had two groups to find in the storm.

CHAPTER ELEVEN

"Where did Midnight go, Mac? I saw him over there." Jamie pointed to an empty spot they had just approached.

"I saw it too, Jamie," Jake said. "It disappeared. How did it do that?" Both boys looked to Mac for an answer, which he didn't have, because now that they were at that spot, he could see there were no footprints in the snow.

"I think you boys are imagining things. I didn't see it." He didn't admit that now that he was older, he could barely see past his nose.

They followed the path for a short distance longer, then Jake shouted again. "There's Midnight. I see him."

"Mac, can you see the horse now?" Jamie asked.

This time, Mac did see a dark blur up ahead. He prayed it was indeed Alex's horse.

"Papa's here!" Jamie yelled.

They moved forward, but the wind picked up again, swirling the snow until they couldn't see the horse anymore.

"Where did it go?"

"You'll see it again once the wind stops blowing the blasted snow about us," Mac said, cursing under his breath.

The snow stopped and they all stared, now speechless.

There was nothing there.

Nothing.

The group split up, leaving several guards with Alice and Kyla, including Kyla's favorite guard, Nicol. Alex trusted Nicol to keep the fire going and his daughter warm, transferring her from his own chest to Nicol's before he left.

Logan traveled east, Brodie and Loki traveled west, and Alex headed south. He was glad they'd bought the two carts with them, as they would certainly need one for Alice and Kyla.

And possibly one for Maddie, wherever she was.

What had the woman been thinking, going off on her own? This he truly couldn't comprehend. He understood Mac going after her and why he took the two lads. He knew his sons, they'd have gone after their mother on their own if he hadn't. He would have had to take them.

But why had Maddie gone alone?

His worst fear gripped him, one he'd done his best to keep at bay. Had someone stolen her away?

Had the danger of that threat been the very thing he'd tried to avoid?

Or had his ordering brought this upon them? He should have been more willing to hear out his wife rather than tell her what to do.

His mind returned to the days before they were married, when his propensity to yell to get someone to hear his message had caused problems between them. He hadn't noticed it at the time, but as soon as Alex had yelled, Maddie would spin on her heel and head in the opposite direction. He hadn't noticed it at first, but once one of his brothers called his attention to her movements, he'd realized he was correct.

So he'd made a point to calm his yelling and lower his voice when dealing with Maddie. He didn't recall that he'd yelled his decision at Maddie this time, so why would she be so upset to make such a rash decision?

Then something his brothers had said came back to him. Celestina had said making demands on her always brought her back to living with her father, who had basically imprisoned her. Hadn't Brodie said she cried whenever he barked an order at her?

And Caralyn had said something similar. That being ordered around made her think of her previous life.

He hadn't thought that making a decision would upset Maddie, but he hadn't discussed it with her at all. His fingers rubbed across his jaw. He had a faint memory of promising his wife to discuss any major decisions with her.

His father had told him it was the man's job to make decisions and the woman's job to follow them. But Alex vaguely remembered his mother standing behind his father with her arms crossed and an angry expression on her face when he'd said it.

Was Logan right? Did all women feel as Caralyn and Celestina did?

If so, if his decision had brought Maddie back to her previous life with Kenneth, the memories it conjured for her would not be sweet. In fact, all he had to do was think about the first time he'd seen Maddie, and his blood reacted fiercely, shooting through his body fast enough for him to clench his fists in reaction.

Her body would react more strongly to that memory than his own. Now he understood. She'd made the decision to leave Grant land out of a combination of fear and anger.

A poor combination for decision-making. Perhaps he needed to calm his own thinking before he found his wife.

If he found her in time. That thought made him break out in a cold sweat, certainly abnormal for these weather conditions. He had to find Maddie, Mac, and the twins, and quickly. His anguish grew so great then that he stopped his horse near a clearing on a hill, tipped his head back to stare up at the gray sky filled with snow clouds, and let out a roar unlike any he'd ever released before. He unleashed his pain, his guilt, his worry over his family. He apologized to Maddie over and over again for failing her.

Then he started. Another rider approached him, but Midnight did not startle, instead remaining calm, as if he knew the rider. Still, Alex reached for the hilt of his sword.

"I'm not here to fight you," the man said, chuckling.

Alex paused. He had never seen the man before, though he looked vaguely familiar. He had long black hair, gray eyes that locked onto his, and a strong profile. It was almost as if Alex were looking at himself at a young age.

"Who are you?"

"Alasdair is my name. You've taught me something just now. I know where I get that tendency to yell when I don't know what else to do," the man said, smiling.

Alex felt his brow furrow. What was the man speaking of?

"What do you want? I cannot waste my time with you," he said, tugging the reins so that Midnight led him away from the odd man.

"I know where she is," the man spoke as Alex prepared to gallop away.

Alex paused. Had he heard him wrong? "Who?"

"Maddie. I'm here to take you to her. You do not have much time." The man crossed his arms; he had an impressive presence.

Alex ignored him, unable to believe the man knew his wife. He turned his horse around and left the man, but it wasn't to be.

A few moments later Alasdair was riding abreast of him. "Maddie. I know where your wife is. I'll take you to her if you'll stop being stubborn and listen."

A blonde woman with a bow across her back suddenly appeared not far away from them, her eyes as blue as Maddie's. "Alasdair, we must hurry."

Alex stopped his horse and stared at her. "Where did you come from?"

He swore that she had not been there the moment before.

"We don't have time for this. Follow us to your wife."

Alex turned back to Alasdair. "Who the hell are you, and who is she?"

"He'll not budge until we tell him, Dyna. You know he's infamous for his stubbornness."

The woman—Dyna—sighed and merely replied with a "Hurry."

Alasdair turned back to Alex. "We are your grandchildren and we are acting as guardian angels. We were allowed to come and help you because Dyna wishes to be born and I wish to know my grandmama. If you don't hurry, Dyna will never exist. She's to be the daughter of your yet unborn son."

Alex just stared at Alasdair, unable to comprehend the words he'd spoken. Grandchildren?

"Jake will be my sire."

His three-year-old son Jake? That's exactly who Alasdair looked like. Jake. The eyes were the same. Alex did not understand how this could be. But suddenly, it didn't matter. He had to find Maddie.

"Come," Dyna said, as if hearing his thoughts. "We cannot wait. You must follow us."

"Where is she?" He followed them because he knew not where else to go.

Alasdair said, "She's in a cave, dying. We sent illusions of your horse to pull Mac and the lads to the same place. Hopefully, they'll arrive about the same time we do."

Alex did not understand half of what they said, but he had to trust his gut on this one. And it told him that these people could take him to his wife. "Take me there and hurry."

Alasdair glanced over his shoulder at him. "You should know you were not wrong, Grandda, about refusing to travel to Ramsay land. There will be a big avalanche from this snowstorm. Had you agreed to come and left in a few days with Logan as planned, it could have buried you all. 'Tis why Grandmama—Maddie—followed her gut and left on her own so suddenly. She felt it her only window of opportunity—and it was."

Dyna smiled and said, "Do not blame her overmuch. We pushed her to leave then, knowing that she'd win you over in the end."

He'd lost his mind, if he were to guess, staring at these apparitions in front of him. But then, he'd been in desperate need of guidance, and there were some things a Scot never questioned.

They flew across the landscape, and he didn't pass another soul along the way, so he had no way of knowing if the two with him were real or not. He supposed it did not matter as long as they brought him to his wife.

A short time later, the lass led them off the main path toward a hidden cave. "She is in there."

She dismounted, pulled on the reins of Alex's horse, and tied them to a bush. He dismounted and rushed into the cave, Alasdair behind him.

"The others will be here soon. They've gone off to direct the others here. Your lads are grand.

It is Grandmama you must help."

There Maddie was, curled up by a dying fire, looking small against the backdrop of the cave. Alex knelt in front of her, Dyna behind him, as Alasdair attended to the fire. His hand went to his wife's cheek, and he was surprised at how cold she was. Should she not be warm near a fire?

He set his hand on her neck to feel for the rhythmic pulse of her heart, but he couldn't find it. He tried the other side of her neck and thought he felt just a wisp of a pulsing beat. "Is she dead?"

"She will be soon if you do not help her. We cannot keep her alive. You must. All we can do is guide you in the right direction. She is too cold. Even the fire is not helping her. Something is going on inside her mind—something we cannot tell—so tread carefully with your words."

"I don't understand what that means." Alex would do anything at this moment for his wife, but he didn't wish to hurt her more, either. He needed guidance.

"She's losing her strength, her will. The will to live is everything. Speak to her. Bring her back."

"Maddie," he whispered, then said it louder when she didn't respond. "Maddie."

Still no response.

"You must give her your heat."

"What?"

"Pick her up. Take her into your arms," Dyna said. "We built a fire, but she needs your heat inside, too. It is why she has not warmed enough."

He did what Dyna said, picking up his wife, the fear of losing her gripping him so hard that he would believe anything these apparitions told him. "Help me. Tell me what to do. Anything. I'll do anything."

"Warm her. She needs to know it is you. You are much of her strength. It comes from you."

Alex wrapped his arm around Maddie and held her tight, closing his eyes to take in her scent. "I'm so sorry, Maddie. Do not leave me yet. Please. Wake up. Yell at me. Anything. I promise I'll listen to you always. I may not agree, but we'll compromise. Please."

Nothing.

"Tell me what to do," he said to Dyna. "I don't know what else to do."

"Give her your heat. Your breath. Your verra will in that breath. The storm drained her will. She is tied to you. Only you can bring her back."

He stared at her, not sure he understood.

Alasdair moved next to Dyna. "Hurry, we don't have much longer. We are only given a short time to do our work."

"Dyna?"

"Place your lips against hers. Part her lips and kiss her so she knows it is you. Your bond should do the rest."

He did what she suggested, setting his lips against Maddie's cold ones, tears filling his eyes at how limp she was, this woman who could be fire in his arms, who could light up his entire being with just a look, whose sweet touch could shoot passion through him as nothing else did.

Limp, nearly dead, not responding.

Alasdair stepped back. "We have to go, Grandsire, but don't give up. She's fighting on the inside."

Dyna reached for Maddie's arm and grasped it tightly, her body taking on a glow and a warmth that made Alex sit back to stare at her, her gaze locked on his. "Don't stop. She will come back to you."

Then Dyna and Alasdair faded away right in front of his eyes.

Alex was frozen for a moment, staring at the empty space where they'd been, before he startled into action. He set his lips against Maddie's again, but she remained limp.

He shifted, holding her tight against his chest as the sobs he'd been holding inside burst forth. He'd only cried like this one other time in his life, and it felt as if the emotion would swallow him whole.

He buried his face in her hair, crushing her against him as he slid closer to the heat of the fire Alasdair had built. "Maddie, Maddie, please . . . come back to me . . . please, Maddie. I love you, I need you. We have more bairns to bring to life. Bairns and grandbairns and more love to give."

He put his lips to hers again, willing her to wake.

He thought he felt a movement against him, so he stilled. After a moment, he set his lips on hers again, willing her to breathe.

This time her lips did move, slowly melding against his, and the joy in his heart burst inside him. She pushed against him, and he lifted his head, looking at her, praying she would awaken and be strong enough to return. Her eyes fluttered open.

"Alex?"

"Aye, I'm here. I love you, Maddie. Wake up, please."

Her eyes opened but then fluttered shut again.

CHAPTER TWELVE

MAC CLOSED HIS eyes and opened them again. The horse had been there and then disappeared. His eyes were indeed playing tricks on him.

"Lads, where did the horse go?"

"It was there a moment ago, then it disappeared," Jake said, turning around. "Wait, Mac. Behind you. Uncle Logan! 'Tis Uncle Logan and Uncle Brodie and Loki!"

Mac stopped his horse and turned around, then took his mount to the side of the path so he could turn the beast sideways, giving them a better view. "God's teeth, thank the Lord above. You're right, lads. I think 'tis our rescuers finally."

"Mac, you cursed. I heard you," Jamie declared.

"He's old enough to curse, Jamie. Don't be a ninny." Jake pushed his brother's arm.

Brodie came up first, calling out to them, Loki coming to the other side of them. "We've been searching everywhere for you and Maddie, first separately, but now together. Once we met up and discovered we had searched the same areas, we decided this was the best path. Are you all well?"

"Aye, the lads and I are well enough."

Logan joined them. "No Maddie?"

Mac shook his head, his fear growing. The wind made the snow swirl around them.

"Have you seen Alex, Mac?"

"Nay."

"We saw Midnight!"

"I saw Midnight too, but then the beast disappeared." Mac shook his head. "I'm not sure what we saw."

"You saw Midnight nearby?" Logan asked.

"We thought we did, but mayhap our eyes were deceiving us. I've gone this way toward Ramsay land, thinking that was the way Maddie headed, but mayhap I'm wrong. Mayhap she went back to find you or Alex."

Loki said, "I hope she didn't go back that way. There was a huge avalanche. You'll not get through the ravine now. The carts just made it through."

"Carts?" Mac asked, hope blooming inside of him for Alice.

"We brought two carts in case anyone needed it," Brodie said.

"We left Alice at—"

"Aye, we know. We found Alice and Kyla first. Nicol stayed with them, along with a few guards. They started a fire."

"They were fine? Alice was shaking terribly."

"We covered her with furs and set her close to the fire. Alex heated Kyla up, and she fell fast asleep before he left. Don't worry, Nicol will take care of Kyla while Alice warms up."

Relief coursed through Mac. "I'm verra glad to hear it. And now? What do we do?"

Logan said, "We're staying together. This storm could be building again. Perhaps we—"

"Midnight! Look, Uncle! He's up ahead again," Jake yelled, pointing in the direction.

Sure enough, there was the beast again, not far ahead.

Brodie said, "Follow that horse!"

Cold. She'd never been so cold.

She was standing on a frozen loch in the middle of an ice storm, wind blowing her hair. Maddie spun around looking for anyone to help her, to take her away from the cold. But she could see nothing through the whirlwind of snow.

Suddenly, a roar of heat blasted straight at her, warming her so much that she moaned. She pivoted toward the heat source, though she could still see nothing.

Another blast came and she ran toward it. She swallowed the hot air, feeling it inside her mouth, down her throat, and into her chest. The sweet warmth spread throughout her.

She needed more.

Her desire was granted. Another blast of heat.

"I love you, I need you. We have more bairns to bring to life. Bairns and grandbairns and more love to give."

Her eyes flew open at the sound of her husband's voice. "Alex?" But the cold pulled at her again, dragging her down.

"I love you, Maddie. Wake up, please."

She resisted the pull, forcing her eyes open again.

"Alex?" she croaked.

Alex cupped her face, and she saw tears running down his cheeks. Alex never cried. She grasped his arms, knowing she had to hang onto him to survive. "Alex? What happened? Why am I so cold?"

But before he could reply, she remembered everything. She'd taken the bairns and left with Mac and Alice, determined to get to Ramsay Castle for the Yuletide. "Alex, forgive me. I'm so sorry. I endangered everyone."

"Hush, love. We'll not speak of it now. Save your strength. You need to get warm." He scuttled closer to the fire, the heat bringing out a sigh in her, followed by a deep shuddering as her body absorbed the warmth.

"The bairns. Kyla, Jake, Jamie . . ." She searched her surroundings for the children, but they weren't there. She pushed against Alex, trying to sit up. "I must find them . . ."

He lifted his wife and settled her on his lap in a sitting position. "I left Kyla safe with Alice. They are hale and Nicol is with them now. He'll keep the fire burning. Brodie even brought goat's milk for our lassie, and Kyla drank her fill. She's well."

"The lads. Where are the twins?"

Alex rested his chin on the top of her head, wrapping his arms around her tightly. "I don't know. Mac went after you and took the lads with him. But fear not—Brodie and Logan are searching the area for them. You know our boys; they'll not be out there quietly."

"What have I done?" She pushed against him, trying to stand. "Alex, we must go after them. We must."

Alex stood, helping her to find her way to her feet, though her knees buckled twice. "What happened to me? Why can I not stand? Where are the laddies? What have I done, Alex? Help me, please."

She fell against him, tears flooding her face in fear. Alex could find them. He would. He must. "Leave me. You must go after them."

"Nay, I'll not leave you. I nearly lost you. Do you know how cold you were when I found you? I thought you were dead, Maddie. If not for . . ." He stopped, an odd look crossing his face. "It does not matter now. But I'll not risk your life. I'll trust my brother and Logan."

He helped her to the entrance of the cave. They stared out at the stunning beauty the storm had left behind: the tree branches covered with snow, the landscape sparkling like crystal whenever the sun peeked out of the clouds.

A sound caught her attention. "Listen, Alex. I heard something."

Sure enough, a moment later came a group of horses headed straight toward them.

Though a good distance away from them, Maddie could still hear her lads. "Papa! Here we come. Is Mama there?"

"I see Mama too."

"I saw her first."

"Nay, I did."

Mac brought his horse up to the cave and whispered, "Thank the Lord above. You're hale, lass?"

Maddie nodded, watching Jamie jump from Mac's horse while Brodie dropped Jake down. The two raced to greet their mother and father.

"Lads, do not soak your mother with your snow. Shake it off your mantles first." Alex pointed over to the side of the cave.

Logan waited until the greetings ended before giving Alex an odd look. "Where's Midnight, Grant?"

"On the far side of the cave. In a covering where he won't get drenched. Why do you ask?"

"He was a big help guiding us here. I wondered why he wasn't here now."

"I don't understand. What do you mean he guided you here?"

"Papa, we saw him. He led us here," Jake said. "Jamie saw him too."

Brodie said, "Aye, he was there, then he disappeared. He kept moving, but each time he was closer to this cave."

Alex looked from one face to the other and said, "Midnight hasn't moved. He's been there since I arrived."

Logan narrowed his gaze at Alex, then shrugged. "Must have been a ghost horse, then."

Brodie chuckled and waved his hand in dismissal.

But Maddie had a sudden memory then of four

riders on horses in the snow—three men and a woman.

Their grandchildren.

CHAPTER THIRTEEN

WHEN THEY FINALLY arrived on Ramsay land, Alex's relief washed through him. With help from his clan, they'd arrived safely, just barely after the sun had set. Maddie was asleep against him, so he didn't awaken her, instead checking on their bairns. Jake, who had been riding with Logan, had already bounced off their mount, Logan dropping directly behind him. Jamie sat in front of Brodie, and they were approaching from behind.

Kyla sat with Nicol, wrapped inside his mantle with her head peeking out of the top. Her eyes widened in the light of the torches around the entrance to Ramsay Castle. Celestina and Inga, Nicol's wife, had come with the second group and caught up to them. It would be a merry time together.

Quade came out with his two bairns, Torrian and Lily, Brenna not far behind them. His sister's voice was as happy as Alex had ever heard her. "I'm so glad you decided to come, Alex! Though I didn't expect you to arrive after dark."

"We had no choice, Brenna. We'll explain later. First we need to get inside and warm everyone up," Alex said, trying his best not to awaken Maddie.

Their youngest sister, Jennie, came running up to the group. At eleven winters, she was the babe of the Grant family. "You made it! And Brodie is here with Loki. And Robbie?"

Logan held his hand up to stop the group chattering. "Robbie's not coming. We've come through a challenging storm in the mountains, so if you could save your questions until later, we'd appreciate it." He looked at Brenna. "Brenna, Alice and Maddie could use some care."

Alex's sister's face changed immediately, transforming her into the healer that she was so well known to be. She began fussing and giving instructions to anyone who would listen to her.

She approached Alex, but he brushed her off. "Maddie is in better shape than Alice now. I've been able to keep her warm. Tend to Alice first. They were alone in the cold for too long. I'll carry Maddie inside."

Logan walked to the cart that carried Mac and Alice, reached inside, and lifted out Alice, who awakened with a start. "We are home?"

"Not home, but Ramsay Castle, Alice," Mac explained.

"As long as there is a hearth inside, I don't mind where we are."

Mac climbed out of the cart and nodded to Logan, indicating for him to take Alice into the warmth of the castle. "Would you take her inside,

Logan? I'll get our bags."

Alex carried Maddie inside, surprised that she didn't wake. Brenna pointed to the chamber at the end of the great hall. "My healing chamber."

She led the way, he with Maddie and Logan following with Alice. Brenna gave instructions to the serving maids as she moved, and Jennie trailed behind her.

"Warm broth in a pitcher, please. Also a basin of hot water and bring two night rails. They're probably both wet and cold. And bring a loaf of bread."

Alex carried Maddie to a pallet and set her carefully on the bed, kissing her forehead; he didn't like the warmth he felt there. "Hellfire."

"What is it, Alex?" Brenna asked, rushing to his side. "What happened to her?"

"She was in a cave alone—do not ask me to tell the tale now—and when I found her, she was barely breathing. I warmed her, set her near a fire, and she did awaken, but she is still weak, Brenna. And I think she is starting a fever."

"Aye, she does feel a little warm."

"The cold—cold like that—it can drain the body. She was fighting to regain her warmth. Still is. Even with the fever."

"Is she wet?"

"Nay, I've kept her dry."

Brenna nodded. "Set her down and cover her with the fur. I'll see to Alice, then I'll be right back. I think I know exactly what she needs."

His sister left the chamber, but not before speaking with Logan and Mac, who had just walked through the door. "My thanks, Logan, but you can leave after you bank the fire in the hearth. Mac, get Alice out of those clothes and into a dry night rail. Jennie can help you. Cover her with the furs, and I'll be right back."

Alex watched the bustle in the healing chamber as Jennie followed their sister's instructions, helping Mac change Alice's clothing. Alex turned around, giving Alice his back so she wouldn't be self-conscious. Then he looked again at Maddie, watching her chest rise and fall. He couldn't help but wonder why Alice was awake and Maddie wasn't. Maddie was so much younger than Alice; she should have fared much better, yet she still slept.

Brenna returned with a babe in her arms and Kyla next to her. "Come see your auntie, Bethia." Then she looked at Alex and said, "We must wake Maddie up and get her to drink some broth. I'm counting on the lassies to inspire her."

Kyla climbed up onto the pallet next to her mother and sat down. "Mama?"

Bethia had been born in the middle of the year, so she wasn't sitting well on her own just yet. Brenna set Bethia on Maddie's belly, face down, and Bethia did just what Brenna hoped she would do. She pushed herself up with her hands until she was looking straight at Maddie.

Kyla got excited and touched Bethia's face, giggling with excitement. "Bairn?"

"'Tis true, Kyla. She's a wee bairn, but you're not any longer. You're a big lassie now." Brenna stayed close, her hand on Bethia's back in case

Maddie awakened. Bethia drooled all over Maddie, and she laughed with Kyla, the two enjoying their time together.

Even Alex had to smile.

Maddie's eyes opened, and she stared at Bethia, then at Kyla, Brenna, and finally at him. "Alex?"

"Maddie, we're at Ramsay Castle for the holiday, just as you wished. Now you must awaken and regain your strength to enjoy it." Alex squeezed her hand. "I'll help you sit up. Kyla can sit with you, and we'll find some broth to help warm your insides."

"Oh, look at this beautiful little girl of yours, Brenna." Maddie ran her hand over the dark hair on Bethia's head as if she were her own. "She's adorable. So lovely."

Tears misted her eyes then, and with her voice heavy with remorse, she said, "To think I nearly didn't . . . the danger I put my own—"

"Nay." Alex decided he couldn't allow her to descend into guilt. Such a feeling would not allow her to improve. "All is well now. These are happy times."

"Alex, I—"

"Truly, Maddie. We've come for the holidays. Think, so many of us together. Now you must do what Brenna advises you to do. You must heal, Maddie."

"I promise, I will."

Alex helped Maddie to a sitting position, then lifted Kyla and placed her on the bed beside her. Jennie ran to get her a cup of broth.

"Alex, I know you do not want me to think on

it too much, and I will not, but you must allow me to say I'm sorry."

"Maddie—"

"I made a huge mistake. I should have listened to you." She looked up at him. "Will you ever forgive me for endangering so many of us?"

While he wished to chastise her for going off alone, he couldn't help but think of the blonde woman who'd told him they'd pushed Maddie to leave. Was it possible that there were angels or some powerful beings who could affect their actions? What had they called themselves? Guardian angels. They'd guided them all to safety in the middle of a snowstorm.

On the way to Ramsay land, he and Mac had discussed a few of the oddities, especially that of his horse Midnight. As far as Alex knew, the horse had remained where he'd left the beast. Surely he'd have seen it move.

"Ach, Maddie. Who knows the true way of things, sweeting? I nearly gave in to your demands. And if we'd have left when I wished to leave, we could have been buried by an avalanche. Your gut instinct was wiser than mine. If we were going to go, we needed to leave when you chose to leave. We'll not talk on it again, but I'll hold to my promise."

She gave him a puzzled look.

"In the cave, when you wouldn't wake, I spoke of all the bairns we had yet to bring into this world. I now remember that promise we made together all that time ago to make big decisions together. You are my wife, and we should work together. I should not always order you about. I have much to learn as a husband."

"And I, as a wife." She tugged on him to pull him down for a kiss. "I love you, Alex, and you are a wonderful husband. We'll work on it together. I was not thinking clearly."

Jennie reappeared with a steaming cup in her hand. "Here you go, Maddie. Mayhap once you're feeling stronger, we can decorate together for the Yule."

"I'd love that, Jennie," she said, before taking a sip of the warm vegetable broth.

Kyla climbed into Maddie's lap and settled against her with her thumb in her mouth. Maddie looked up at him. "Alex, I'll be fine. Why don't you check on the lads? Make sure they're eating something. They didn't have much to eat when we were traveling."

"Verra well, Maddie." He leaned down and kissed her cheek, then Kyla's forehead. "I'll return after I see to the laddies."

***

Maddie sat in a chair near the hearth just before the evening meal on the first day of Yule, reveling in the happiness bubbling out of her in the moment. Her family was making their way inside for the meal, including her husband, who found his way to her side. Tonight would be their family meal, on the morrow there would be a big feast for all the villagers.

The holiday had been near perfect, if not for the way it had begun. But no one had said a word about Maddie's lack of judgment after the first day they arrived. And they'd all thrown themselves into the festivities.

Earlier, the twins had been building forts in the snow, rolling down hills, and enjoying play time with Torrian and Lily. Maddie and Brenna had helped make a whole bundle of apple pastries and pear tarts, and Jennie had helped, mostly so she could sample each batch. It'd been a wonderful sennight.

Brenna approached her and Alex. "How are you faring tonight, Maddie?"

"Well, Brenna. Though I still find myself desiring sleep more oft than I should."

Brenna smirked like she had a secret. "You do think you're carrying, do you not, Maddie?"

Maddie blinked, struck silent for a moment, and Breanna laughed.

"The desire for rest, the need for sleep—'tis a sign of a babe. Many women feel so in the early days, when a new bairn is starting out and even beyond."

Her hand went to her belly. "Aye, I'm quite sure."

Truth be told, she was certain she carried their fourth child, but she wasn't ready to tell the others before she spoke to Alex. She'd decided to do so tonight, when they were alone, so for now she'd feign uncertainty to Brenna.

"Will it please you if you are?"

She glanced at her husband. "Aye, we did want more bairns."

Alex grinned, nodding in agreement.

"And what do you think you'll have this time, if it's true? Another lassie?"

Maddie and Alex answered in unison. "Nay, another lad."

Brenna gave the two of them an odd look, then brushed it off. "If it is a lad, mayhap you'll name this one Alexander or Alasdair. Were you not considering those had Kyla been a boy?"

Alex whispered, "Nay. Connor, I think."

Maddie felt a jolt at the name and turned to Alex with a question on her face.

But Alex only scratched his head and shrugged. "Just came to me, Maddie."

The door opened with a bang then, interrupting their conversation. Logan came in with Gwyneth, a fat goose in his hand. "My Gwynie caught another for the morrow's dinner. With the small deer Alex brought, we've venison and goose for the week. We'll eat hearty and with plenty for all."

A cheer arose at Logan's announcement, and that's when Maddie noticed there was a distinct lack of bairns gathered inside. They had to be planning something, with Loki, Torrian, Molly, and Maggie probably guiding the younger ones.

As if they'd heard her thoughts, the crew came barreling down the staircase, the twins in the lead. Jake ran to her and leaned on her knees, his face full of excitement as he looked up at her. "Mama, wait until you see our play after dinner."

Jamie said, "'Tis great. You'll love our parts."

"I cannot wait to see it, lads, but first we must eat."

They all moved to the long table, and serving lasses brought out trenchers of thick beef stew, full of carrots and barley, then loaves of bread and some mutton meat pies. They ate heartily, enjoying the scrumptious meal, most of them eating quietly except for Kyla's occasional outburst.

She would point to the corner near the hearth and announce, "Angels."

"Aye, sweetie, 'tis the night for angels." Maddie had talked with Kyla about the Lord and angels and even the holidays, just as her mother had done with her many years ago.

Once they finished their meal, the lads jumped off the trestle table and helped Loki and Torrian push the chairs and stools near the hearth, making space for their play.

Alex took a seat next to Maddie, taking her hand and tucking it inside his large one. He whispered, "Did they tell you what the play was?"

"Nay, it will be a surprise."

Loki came out first and announced, "'Tis the time of last summer, when the Norsemen and King Haakon fought their way up the firth to try to gain Scotland for Norway."

Then he stepped back and Torrian said, "Let the battle begin!"

The lads charged out on their pretend horses, fighting the imaginary Norsemen with their swords, though the wooden hilts were nearly broken from all the use they got. Loki used his pretend slinger, imitating exactly how he'd used it in the battle. Molly and Maggie played the Norse, eventually falling to the ground, defeated by the Scots.

Torrian came on stage then and imitated his uncle Logan, and Loki became Brodie with his injured leg. They played the story out just as it had been told many times over, Brodie so sick over not being near Celestina that he didn't wish to go home so his sister could fix his leg after battle. Then Torrian pretended to strike Loki with his fist, just as Logan had truly done to Brodie to get him home.

Celestina laughed and teased her husband, while Brodie sheepishly looked around at the rest of the crowd. "I was in love and badly injured."

The play ended on that note, and players all came out to take a bow. The crowd applauded and the group broke apart.

Maddie looked about her and asked Alex, "Where did Kyla go?"

"She went over to a basket in the corner by the door."

A few seconds later, Kyla rushed over with her unsteady run, holding something up for her mother. It was wrapped in fabric, so Maddie took it and opened it, surprised to see a new sword styled just for Kyla's size.

The lass claimed it quickly. "Mine."

"Kyla, where did you get this?"

She pointed to the basket in the corner.

Jamie and Jake walked over, quickly noticing Kyla's sword. "New swords? Do we get one?"

They looked up at their parents, expecting to be handed gifts.

Maddie said, "Lads, we came in a rush. I did

not bring any gifts. We barely made it here in the storm."

"But Kyla got one!"

Kyla pointed over to the basket once again.

The twins spotted the basket then, and they raced across the floor. Loki and Torrian noticed the commotion and ran over too.

Maddie looked at Alex and they quickly followed the children.

Torrian was peering into the basket when they arrived. "Papa? Where did this come from?"

Quade walked over, peeked into the large basket, and said, "I know not. It's full of wrapped gifts. Come, let us bring it into the center of room, and we'll see what they are."

Quade and Loki pulled the large basket over together. Now most of the family crowded around the basket, curious. Quade took out a package wrapped with fabric and twine and tried to hand it to Jennie, but Kyla shouted, "'Olly! 'Olly!"

Quade paused, turning to the wee lassie. "Molly?"

"Aye!"

Quade shrugged and handed the package to Molly.

They all waited while she opened it, her mouth forming a perfect circle when she lifted the present out of the cloth. "I've always wanted a lute!"

Quade turned to Kyla in astonishment. "Verra well, lassie, you tell me who to give these to."

And so it continued: Quade would hold each one out to Kyla, and she would point to whomever she wished to give the gift to, waiting for each person to open it.

Maggie received new leggings, Torrian got a new sword, as did the lads, and Loki got a special slinger crafted unlike anything they'd ever seen.

"Alex, what is happening? How does our wee lassie know who gets each gift?"

The basket seemed to be bottomless. Alex received a golden broach for his kilt, Maddie a gold necklace with the Grant crest in the center. Quade, Brenna, Brodie, Celestina, Logan, and Gwyneth all received a gift as well.

Everyone was in awe. When the basket was finally empty, Quade said, "Thank you, Alex and Maddie."

"'Twas lovely of you to bring the gifts," Brenna echoed.

Maddie shook her head. "We didn't. I thought you had."

"Nay, we did not. Brodie?"

Brodie shook his head.

"Logan and Gwyneth?" The two denied leaving the gifts.

Quade looked to Alex and said, "What do you make of it?"

"I don't know. Perhaps someone in the village is responsible, and you'll find out on the morrow when you have the clan feast."

Quade scowled but then slowly nodded. "Mayhap you are correct."

Kyla looked up at her uncle, held her tiny hands out, and said, "Up."

Quade lifted her high in the air, tossing her above his head and sending her into a fit of giggles.

Brenna said, "It was Kyla that brought the first gift out. Ask her who brought the basket."

"Do you know, you wee trickster?" Quade asked, laughing at her.

When Kyla finally stopped giggling, she nodded at Quade.

"Who then, lassie?" Maddie asked.

"Angels."

CHAPTER FOURTEEN

THE DAY AFTER the festival, Alex had sought the quiet of the castle parapets after waking. He'd been observing the land for a time when he heard someone climbing the stairs behind him. He turned to see who would be joining him, surprised to see his dear wife coming through the door. "'Tis a bit cool up here for you, Maddie."

"I know, but I have my own hearth to keep me warm." She wrinkled her nose at her husband, grabbing his upper arm with a smile.

He chuckled, knowing exactly what she meant, and opened his arms to her. She tucked herself against his large frame. She was so small and delicate, except when it came to her character, which was equal parts stubborn and strong.

He kissed the top of her head and asked, "Have you something on your mind?"

"I do, and I wished to discuss it where no one else could overhear us."

"Then you found the perfect spot. What is it you wish to discuss?"

He asked the question and then fell silent, giving her time to gather her thoughts. He guessed it was something important to her if it brought her to the cold of the Ramsay parapets.

"I'm not sure how to ask this properly, so I'll simply say it: I have some odd memories from when I was in the cave. And in the snow. I thought I might have fallen asleep on the horse and it led me to the cave, but the fire . . . Yet the way I remember it—these memories—couldn't possibly have happened. It must have been a dream. Perhaps in my delirium, I lit a fire. I . . . I am not certain."

She waited, glancing up at him.

He wasn't sure how to answer her. He'd thought of his own odd experience that day, how he'd been on the top of a hill, shouting at the world over all that had happened, and then two people had popped up out of nowhere.

They'd said they were his grandchildren.

But he wasn't ready to admit his visions yet.

"Tell me what you think you saw, and I'll help you understand it, if 'tis possible. But I'll warn you, there are some things that cannot be easily explained—at least, not in Scotland. My mother was a true believer of the faeries, for one."

Maddie cleared her throat, a habit of hers when she was nervous. "I was lost in the storm, the snow swirling around me, confusing me. I didn't know which way to go. I closed my eyes for a moment, and when I opened them, four riders were leading me forward. One had the reins of my horse. They took me to the cave where you found me, built a fire, covered me in furs, fed me, and took care of my horse."

"You didn't know them?"

"Nay."

"Did they tell you what clan they were from? Or do you recall what plaid they wore under their mantles?"

"They were wearing Grant plaids. I saw the red and the black. They didn't say so, but I saw it. They only told me their first names."

"Then you must have recognized them if they were from Clan Grant. At least one?"

"I didn't recognize them . . . but . . . one looked truly familiar . . ." She fell silent again.

An odd feeling crept up his spine, spreading out to his limbs, making the hairs of his arms stand on end. "The one who looked familiar . . ."

"Looked like you, Alex. The hair, the gray eyes, your height or nearly so. Just something about him."

"And his first name?"

Her voice came out in a whisper. "Alasdair."

Glad she wasn't looking at him, he nearly choked at the name. It was the same man, then.

"And the names of the others?"

She cleared her throat again. "Els and Alick. The fourth was a lass. A beautiful lass."

Alex felt a lump in his throat, knowing what Maddie would say . . .

"She was named Dyna."

Alex stepped back, releasing Maddie, and leaned against the hard stone wall of the castle next to the doorway.

Maddie whirled around to stare at him.

It couldn't be. Could it?

Alex reached for her hand and whispered, "I met Alasdair and Dyna."

Her eyes widened. "You did? And Els and Alick?"

"Nay. Just Alasdair and Dyna."

She tipped her head in question at him.

"They guided me to you, led me to the cave. I was so upset, I could not think clearly. I didn't know how to help you. Dyna told me what to do. But after, I thought I'd merely lost my mind with worry. I'd thought you were dead, and it drove me to madness. But now . . ." He paused, closing his eyes as if to lock in the memory of the two, what they looked like, their voices, the way they carried themselves. "Did they tell you anything odd?"

Maddie gulped three times, glancing back over her shoulder as if to make sure no one had joined them. "Aye. They said they were—"

"Our grandchildren," he finished with her.

A sudden laugh, high and nervous, escaped from Maddie, and she slapped a hand over her mouth. Alex let out his breath in a loud whoosh.

They'd both met their grandchildren.

The implications of her words astounded him. They couldn't have imagined the same thing, not with the same details.

"Alex?"

"Alasdair didn't look like me," Alex found himself saying.

"Aye, he did."

"Nay, he looked like our son, Maddie. Jake. He's

Jake's son. The eyes were exactly the same. He said Jake was his sire."

"I do not understand how this is possible, Alex."

"Nor I. But there is much we do not understand. The Highlands have their magick, their faeries, other odd events, aye? Mayhap this is one of them."

"I struggled with this memory, Alex, and was ready to dismiss it because of my illness, the storm . . . The entire event was so unusual for us."

"Agreed. I swore I would not mention it to anyone, but knowing you experienced a similar situation with some of the same people . . . It forces me to consider it to be true. All of it. Do you not agree?" He glanced at her, hoping she would agree with him and not consider him daft.

"Aye." Maddie looked away, toward the forest, then met his eyes again.

"We should probably not tell anyone else. Would they believe us?"

Alex snorted. "Nay, we must keep it our secret. No one would believe us."

She nodded her head in agreement as she stared at her hands, then brought her face back up to look at him, a sudden inspiration showing on her face that made him wonder what more she could possibly have recalled.

"Did Dyna tell you who her sire was?"

Alex nodded. "Our unborn son."

"Aye, she said 'twas why she came to us. She couldn't allow me to die, or she wouldn't be born. She said her sire was in my belly now."

Alex couldn't hide the surprise on his face.

"She did not tell me that."

She nodded. "It was part of what I came to tell you, Alex. I'm sure now. I'm sure I'm carrying." She grabbed his hand. "'Tis another laddie, Alex. We're to have another son."

He smiled. "What shall we name him?" Alex asked the question already knowing what his own answer would be. The name had been bouncing inside his skull for days, since he'd first uttered it in front of Maddie and Brenna. He knew not why, only that it was.

Maddie sent him a look. "You've already said, Alex. Dyna told me the same."

"Verra well." He placed a hand on Maddie's stomach. "Hello, Connor Grant."

It was the last day of their holiday journey, and Logan had promised to take all the young ones to the loch so they could slide across the ice. He'd been out testing the ice to make sure it could hold their weight, and the twins had nearly exploded waiting inside for the final approval.

When it came, the group traveled on horseback and made it to the loch in less than a quarter hour. Maddie stood with Alex while they watched the twins shriek and giggle on the ice that Logan had swept clear, Kyla waddling around them.

Alex wrapped his arms around his wife from behind, protecting her from the light wind and nuzzling her neck. "You'll not sneak out ahead of me this time, will you, lass?"

Maddie wasn't surprised he made that statement, so she answered him honestly. "Alex, I meant it before. I promise never to do it again. It was poor judgment on my part, and I admit it."

"Good. It was sheer torture for me." He paused. "And I'll keep my promise as well. I'll discuss my decisions with you and keep an open mind."

"Good." Maddie smiled. "We have had a wonderful time, have we not?"

"Aye, I have enjoyed it verra much. My sister did provide a mighty fine feast. And to be gathered together in the great hall with the bairns' voices ringing out did well for my spirits. Though I do miss Robbie and his family."

"True, but at least you know the castle is guarded well."

Kyla took off running toward a group of trees, in the opposite direction of the loch. "'Tis the third time she's tried this," Alex grumbled. "What do you suppose she's after?"

"One can never know the direction of a wee bairn's mind," Maddie replied over her shoulder as she chased Kyla, watching the excitement on her face as she tried to escape Maddie's clutches. Maddie scooped her up in her arms. "Nay, you'll not get away from me, lassie. Who knows what animal is in the woods?"

Kyla responded quickly and stronger than Maddie had ever seen her do. "Nay, down."

Alex caught up with them. "Nay, you come with Mama and Papa."

"Nay." She scowled, something that made both of them chuckle. At nearly a year and a half old, she was a stubborn lass.

Alex asked, "Why do you want to go? Give us the reason, Kyla, and we'll consider it."

They were always pushing her language because she was so clever, but neither of them expected her answer.

She pointed into the trees and said one word. "Angel."

Alex laughed, but Maddie stopped, looking into the trees with new consideration. "What did you say, Kyla?"

"Angel."

Could it be?

Maddie looked at Alex. "An angel, Alex. Mayhap we know this one."

Alex must have caught on to her meaning, for his gaze shot to the trees, searching.

Maddie looked back at her daughter. "Did the angel have a name, Kyla?"

"Dyna."

Maddie's gaze shot to Alex.

"Set her down and let her go. I wish to see where she goes."

"Alex . . ."

"We're here. 'Tis safe."

Maddie set Kyla down. "Go ahead, Kyla. Show us."

Kyla waddled into the woods, the two of them on her heels. Once they were inside the cover of trees, Kyla stopped and waved.

Out from behind a tree came the form of a woman. Dressed in black leggings, boots, and a dark tunic, Dyna stepped forward. Her long white-blond hair was plaited down her back, and a bow was over her shoulder.

Kyla said, "Bye-bye, Dyna." Her little hand came up and waved furiously.

"Goodbye, Kyla. Be good for Mama and Papa." She waved to the wee lass, who giggled, her hand still waving.

"You were the angel she's been speaking of? The one who left the basket of gifts?"

"Aye, the young can connect with us easier than the elders, so I told Kyla to get her gift."

Dyna took her gaze from the lass and looked at Alex and Maddie. "Don't worry. We'll keep an eye on her. She'll have her moments, but she'll bring you much joy over the years."

"We?" Alex whispered.

"Alasdair, Alick, Els, and I. We'll watch over all of you."

Neither Maddie nor Alex could speak, so they just watched the angel as she picked up Kyla, kissed her cheek, then set her back down.

"'Tis the way it works. If we're not with you, we watch over you. There are many more angels from your clan watching over our loved ones, but you know us all one way or another." She laughed. "But you've given us many to watch, and there will be more. At least two more."

Then she turned on her heel and strode away from them, her plait swinging back and forth.

"Bye, Dyna," Kyla said.

Dyna stopped and blew Kyla a kiss, making the bairn giggle.

"Love you both, Grandsire and Grandmama," she said, an odd catch in her throat.

Then Dyna disappeared, but her voice continued to carry to them through the trees. "Miss you, but I'll see you soon."

THE END

www.keiramontclair.com

DEAR READER,
Thank you for reading about my Christmas Angels going on another journey where things are not always as they seem, the mystical can confuse us, and you sometimes just have to believe in something that seems impossible.

If you haven't met Alasdair, Els, Alick, and Dyna, then you need to read the Highland Swords series. It begins with Alasdair's story.

I wish you all the most happy and healthy holiday season.

Keira Montclair

www.keiramontclair.com

NOVELS BY KEIRA MONTCLAIR

THE CLAN GRANT SERIES
#1- RESCUED BY A HIGHLANDER-
Alex and Maddie
#2- HEALING A HIGHLANDER'S HEART-
Brenna and Quade
#3- LOVE LETTERS FROM LARGS-
Brodie and Celestina
#4-JOURNEY TO THE HIGHLANDS-
Robbie and Caralyn
#5-HIGHLAND SPARKS-
Logan and Gwyneth
#6-MY DESPERATE HIGHLANDER-
Micheil and Diana
#7-THE BRIGHTEST STAR IN THE HIGHLANDS-
Jennie and Aedan
#8- HIGHLAND HARMONY-
Avelina and Drew
#9-YULETIDE ANGELS

THE HIGHLAND CLAN
LOKI-Book One
TORRIAN-Book Two
LILY-Book Three
JAKE-Book Four
ASHLYN-Book Five

MOLLY-Book Six
JAMIE AND GRACIE-Book Seven
SORCHA-Book Eight
KYLA-Book Nine
BETHIA-Book Ten
LOKI'S CHRISTMAS STORY-Book Eleven
ELIZABETH-Book Twelve

THE BAND OF COUSINS
HIGHLAND VENGEANCE
HIGHLAND ABDUCTION
HIGHLAND RETRIBUTION
HIGHLAND LIES
HIGHLAND FORTITUDE
HIGHLAND RESILIENCE
HIGHLAND DEVOTION
HIGHLAND BRAWN
HIGHLAND YULETIDE MAGIC

HIGHLAND SWORDS
THE SCOT'S BETRAYAL
THE SCOT'S SPY
THE SCOT'S PURSUIT
THE SCOT'S QUEST
THE SCOT'S DECEPTION
THE SCOT'S ANGEL

HIGHLAND HEALERS
THE CURSE OF BLACK ISLE
THE WITCH OF BLACK ISLE
THE SCOURGE OF BLACK ISLE

THE SOULMATE CHRONICLES
#1 TRUSTING A HIGHLANDER
#2 TRUSTING A SCOT

STAND-ALONE BOOKS
THE BANISHED HIGHLANDER
REFORMING THE DUKE-REGENCY
WOLF AND THE WILD SCOTS
FALLING FOR THE CHIEFTAIN-3RD in a collaborative trilogy

THE SUMMERHILL SERIES- CONTEMPORARY ROMANCE
#1-ONE SUMMERHILL DAY
#2-A FRESH START FOR TWO
#3-THREE REASONS TO LOVE

About the Author

Keira Montclair is the pen name of an author who lives in South Carolina with her husband. She loves to write fast-paced, emotional romance, especially with children as secondary characters.

When she's not writing, she loves to spend time with her grandchildren. She's worked as a high school math teacher, a registered nurse, and an office manager. She loves ballet, mathematics, puzzles, learning anything new, and creating new characters for her readers to fall in love with.

She writes historical romantic suspense. Her best-selling series is a family saga that follows two medieval Scottish clans through four generations and now numbers over thirty books.

Contact her through her website:
www.keiramontclair.com

Made in the USA
Middletown, DE
27 December 2024